The man's hair was brushed back, and tied in a tail at the nape of his neck, where it curled a little. He hadn't powdered it, like a fashionable noble, and it shone red-gold in the candlelight. He had hazel eyes that glittered as Colette gazed into them.

'Do you know who I am?' he asked her gently.

'Ma said that you were dead,' Colette murmured. 'If you're who I think you must be...'

'Since she refused to see me, after we parted, I might as well have been,' the man said bitterly. 'She and I did not agree, Colette. On many things, we discovered. But I *am* your father.'

Also by Holly Webb

The Water Horse
The Mermaid's Sister

Rose Series

Rose
Rose and the Lost Princess
Rose and the Magician's Mask
Rose and the Silver Ghost

Lily Series

Lily
Lily and the Shining Dragons
Lily and the Prisoner of Magic
Lily and the Traitor's Spell

The Maskmaker's Daughter

Holly Webb

ORCHARD

ORCHARD BOOKS
First published in Great Britain in 2016 by The Watts Publishing Group

1 3 5 7 9 10 8 6 4 2

A CIP catalogue record for this book is available from the British Library.

ISBN 978 1 40832 766 1

Typeset in Adobe Caslon by Avon DataSet Ltd, Bidford-on-Avon, Warwickshire

Printed and bound in Great Britain by CPI Group (UK) Ltd, Croydon, CR0 4YY

The paper and board used in this book are made from wood from responsible sources.

FSC www.fsc.org MIX Paper from responsible sources FSC® C104740

Orchard Books
An imprint of Hachette Children's Group
Part of The Watts Publishing Group Limited
Carmelite House
50 Victoria Embankment
London EC4Y 0DZ

An Hachette UK Company
www.hachette.co.uk

www.hachettechildrens.co.uk

For Felicity

Chapter One

COLETTE RAN HER FINGERS GENTLY over the silk. She flinched a little as her roughened fingertips caught, and swiftly tucked her hands away in the folds of her skirt. The silk was too precious to risk snagging the threads, but she wanted to touch. She wanted to wrap herself in it and feel the cool blueness shining on her skin.

It shimmered so, glowing blue and green depending on how the light fell, how it was folded, how it shifted when she ran her fingers over its gleaming surface.

But she mustn't, even though she felt as though each thinner-than-hair thread was calling out to her.

The tiny spells she worked with Ma jumped inside her, making her fingers tremble. They were old, worn charms, nothing grand. Just cantrips muttered against knots in the sewing silk or blunted scissors, magic that had been passed on to apprentice after apprentice, to smooth the hard life of a seamstress just a little.

There was a richer magic in the blue silk, Colette was sure. It was from the East, Ma said. It had come off a ship, moored up at the mouth of the Grand Canal. Ma had tried to hustle Colette away as they heard the merchant cursing, but Colette had ducked under her arm. She had seen a glimpse of that shining blue, she told Ma later, but it wasn't true. She had *known* it was there, inside the water-spoiled wrappings. It had called to her. They had bargained with the cloth merchant, who was glad to get something for the spoiled bale of cloth, and carried it home, lugging it along the little *calli* and bridges.

When they'd opened it out, the great salty streaks that had so infuriated the merchant seemed to have seeped away. *The salt water is inside the cloth now*, Colette thought sometimes, looking at the watery dance of the sunlight on the silk.

Oh, the dresses she could make, if the fabric were really hers… It was a waste, that all its colour and life should be buried under crystal embroidery, gold thread and lace.

'Colette!' Her mother's voice broke sharply into her thoughts, and her hands jumped inside the thin cotton of her skirt. 'Colette, stop daydreaming! We don't have time. Put that silk away. Tidy your hair. They'll be here, any moment.'

'I know.' Colette jumped up, and the silk spilled off her lap in a watery mass.

Her mother clucked warningly, and reached out a hand to the precious stuff. Then she leaned back against her chair, caught by a spasm of coughing.

Colette watched her worriedly, standing there with her arms full of silk and hating the way the bones of her mother's shoulders stood out.

'The dust…' her mother whispered at last. 'Only the dust. All these trimmings and scraps and threads, Colette. It all makes dust.'

'I'll sweep it up,' Colette promised eagerly. 'I didn't sweep properly yesterday, that's why you're coughing. And I'll wash the floor, Ma. There'll be no dust left to catch in your throat then, will there?'

'They're coming.' Her mother sprang up, clutching at the back of her chair to steady herself. 'I hear them… Get out to the shop, Colette, you're faster than I am. Don't keep Madame the Countess waiting!'

Colette could hear them too, as she hurried out of the workroom, fixing her face into a subdued grimace of welcome. Madame's page was stomping over the paving stones to hammer on the door, and she flung it open before he could damage the paintwork.

The boy glared at her, and then stood back to usher in his mistress, who was edging irritably through the narrow door. Her dress was wide enough that she had to turn sideways, and her maid was fussing over the satin. Colette didn't recognise the dress – it had come from another tailor. Ma would have sweet-talked the countess away from that heavy patterned stuff. She looked like a walking flowerbed. Even her delicate, gilded mask had jasmine clustered around the eyes.

'Where is your mother, child?' the countess demanded.

'I'm here, my lady.' Colette's mother hurried in, dropping into a curtsey and tugging Colette down with her. Colette tried not to hear the faint wheeze in her mother's chest as they bowed their heads. Ma always blamed the dust, or the constant damp that seeped through the stonework from the canals, or the wood fires they burned to keep the damp off the silks. It was no wonder she coughed, she kept telling Colette. She would be better in the spring. *But it's the spring now!* Colette felt the words rising up inside her, even though she couldn't bear to say them out loud. She could only hope and pray and close her eyes and pretend that Ma would get better.

If the countess ordered a new court costume, Colette could buy the herbs to make a posset for Ma's throat. Some eggs maybe, to make a custard to slip down easy. Colette would even be glad if Countess Morezzi bought the blue silk, though it made her ache inside to think of the workroom without its shimmering blue-green light.

'Would Madame like to see the dolls?' Ma asked hopefully, as she struggled upright. 'We have some entirely new fashions, straight from London. Very select. Very suited to Madame's delicate colouring.'

Colette fought not to let her lips twist into a smirk. They all knew that Madame's delicate colouring came entirely out of the little pots on her dressing table, that Sofie the maid painted on her pretty blush with a rabbit's foot. The countess would be unrecognisable without her towering puffed hair and painted face. *She'd probably look like Ma*, Colette thought, bobbing another curtsey and padding backwards to the shelves to fetch the new English dolls.

The countess peered at them, fingering the fabrics as Ma twittered on about wider panniers, and Chinese painted silk, and double pleated ribbon trimming. The dolls lay limply on Colette's outstretched arms, their faces painted with foolish little rosebud smiles. The countess poked them disapprovingly and her lips twisted in a pettish little smirk. 'The same as everyone else's…' she murmured, and Colette heard her mother's tiny sigh. She was not going to order a new dress. Perhaps Sofie would pick up a pot of rouge, or some ribbons, but there was hardly any money in those. They *needed* a new commission. Ma was one of the best dressmakers in the city, but their tiny shop wasn't grand enough for most of the court nobility. And there were all the whisperings about Ma still. So few of the dressmakers in Venice were women, there was an assumption that Ma could never be as good as a proper tailor. It didn't help that

Colette's father had died soon after she was born. It had taken a long time for the Tailors' Guild to accept Ma for membership.

Colette was quite sure that Countess Morezzi only came to Harriet's because they were cheap, and convenient, in that her family's palazzo was quite close by. And there was still a certain novelty in a London seamstress in Venice. The countess could be seen as fashionably eccentric, patronising such a little, out-of-the-way place.

Colette wanted to plead with her, but there was no chance of that. Ma looked defeated, and more tired than ever as she took the pattern dolls from Colette and laid them gently back in their places. Colette could hear her wheezing again, and she turned back to the countess, curtseying low. 'Would you wait a moment, Madame?' she murmured. 'We have some silk – very special. No one else in the city has anything like it. It would make the most fascinating dress for carnival, my lady.'

'No one else…?' The countess looked sharply at

Colette. 'And why did you not show me this before?'

'It's quite new, my lady,' Ma put in, smiling worriedly at her. 'And very dear… Perhaps only for the most special of dresses.'

Colette sensed the countess stiffen slightly. There was a faint whisper of her satin skirts against the floor, and the silver flowers embroidered on the fabric glittered. Colette stared hard at the floor, twisting her fingers behind her back. Had Ma meant to do that? To suggest that the countess couldn't afford an expensive new dress? Because either now she would storm out and tell everyone that Harriet's was out of date, shoddy and not to be trusted, or she would order that dress, with every little extra that could possibly be squeezed onto it…

'Show me!' the countess demanded, and Colette hurried back into the workroom, gathering up the blue silk with a sharp stab of regret. It slithered over her arms, watery-cool, and she ducked her head to rub it once against her cheek. Then she carried it out to show the countess, who would ruin it with spangles and knots of ribbon, and her pale, fish-like face.

They needed the money. They needed Countess Morezzi to show off one of Ma's dresses. The rent was past due. This had to *work*.

'Show her,' Colette whispered to the blue silk in her arms. '*Please*.' And she felt the shimmering threads tremble and warm against her skin. The silk glistened as she held it out to the countess. 'For carnival, my lady,' Colette murmured. 'Perhaps with a grand headdress. We could make you the ornaments, my lady. Little ships, and – and mermaids…' Her voice whispered to nothing in the silence.

'I could give a ball,' the countess said suddenly. 'A patriotic ball at the palazzo, celebrating our city's mastery of the sea. Yes. With a most extravagant wig… I have something of the kind.' She paced across the tiny showroom, muttering to herself, and then rounded on Ma. 'You will make me this dress, for a springtime ball, before the weather grows too hot. I shall require it in three weeks.'

'Three weeks!' Ma said faintly, and the countess stared down her long nose, like a seagull.

'Indeed.'

Ma nodded, and curtseyed. 'Yes, my lady, three weeks.'

'Send me the drawings. I shall come for a first fitting in a week.' She stroked the silk again, even drawing off one fine kid glove, and nodded. Then she sailed majestically towards the door, so that the little page boy who had been half dozing in the corner had to leap across the room to open it in time, and guide out the absurd mass of her skirts. Then he hurried before her to the water, hastily shooing away a thin cat that had been nosing around the boatman's ankles, and the countess was half pushed, half lifted into the narrow gondola.

Ma stayed staring after her, half dipped in a curtsey, till Colette hauled her up. 'She's taking a dress,' she murmured. 'That silk. Oh, Colette, think of what we can charge.'

'But three weeks! I don't see how—'

'We must.' Ma hugged her, wrapping her arms around Colette tight. 'We can't not, Colette.' She hunted in the little hanging pocket around her waist and pulled out a coin. 'Give me the silk, dear heart, and go and buy some candles. We shall be working late.'

Colette took the coin and went to the door, looking back at Ma cradling the bolt of silk like a baby, and murmuring to it. Perhaps it was only the blue-green glow of the fabric on her skin, but Colette thought she had never seen her look so pale.

Still thinking of Ma, and worrying about three weeks of midnight work by candlelight, Colette hurried heedlessly across the stones, almost tripping over the skinny alley cat as she approached the bridge. The cat dodged out of the way with a hiss that told her quite clearly that she was a blundering fool. Colette, anxious and not thinking, said earnestly, 'I'm so sorry. Are you hurt?'

For a moment, she almost thought the cat would answer, it was staring at her so closely. Then it leaped up onto the balustrade of the tiny bridge, so it could peer even closer.

It wasn't a pretty cat, but it had a certain rakish pirate elegance, with its torn ears and mottled tortoiseshell coat. It had heavy black markings around its eyes, too, almost as if it were wearing a mask.

'I wasn't looking properly. I was worrying about something. I'm very sorry if I trod on your paws.' Colette gazed into the cat's green-gold gooseberry eyes uncertainly, and decided to stop talking, in case the cat *did* answer her. There was something about this creature… It had been hanging around for a while, but Colette had never looked at it this closely before. Its whiskers were black on one side, and white on the other.

Colette swallowed, to wet her dry throat. Everyone in Venice knew that Duchess Olivia's maid had a magical cat, who walked among the court in a silver collar, and was widely believed to be a spy. But even he didn't *talk*. Or at least, not so that anyone heard him.

The cat nodded to Colette, and then sat down, head held high and its tail curled neatly around its paws, as if it were some pampered pet, and not an alley cat at all. Colette nodded back – she couldn't not – and walked across the bridge to the market to buy her tallow candles, with the tortoiseshell cat watching her all the way.

Chapter Two

'Go to bed, Colette. You're yawning. You're half asleep over that stitching as it is.'

'I'm not,' Colette muttered thickly. 'I'm awake, I'm sewing, look.' She peered down at the little golden fish she was embroidering and sighed. The huge stitches were straggling down the fabric like a ladder. She must have been sewing in her sleep. Now she'd have to unpick the mess, and sweet-talk the threads of the silk into closing up all those ugly little holes. 'It's so nearly finished,' she sighed. 'And we need it, to show the countess tomorrow when she comes for the fitting. She'll want to see the pattern. She said…'

'Then you can finish it in the morning.' Ma sighed, and stretched out her cramped fingers. 'Go, Colette. You're only making more work for yourself.' She leaned over and lifted the fabric out of Colette's hands.

'She probably won't come, after all this,' Colette yawned, stumbling up out of her chair.

But Ma shook her head grimly. 'She will. You didn't see her eyes, Colette, when she touched the silk. She wants this dress. There's something about it, this cloth.' She stroked it gently. 'Even I don't want to let it go, sometimes. And I've seen enough silk for a lifetime. I'm not even sure I like the colour. But still…'

'I wish we could keep it. I hate to think of her wearing it.' Colette would never have said the words if she hadn't been so tired, but they slipped out without her meaning to say them.

Her mother was silent for a moment, and Colette dropped her eyes. How many times had Ma told her that the dresses they made were not for the likes of them, ever? That the grand, hoop-skirted dresses they slaved over were a prison, for rich, silly women who could afford to take five minutes to struggle through a doorway? Colette's own clothes were simple, and neat, and plain, and that was as it should be. She would never wear blue watered silk.

'There'll be scraps.'

Colette looked up, surprised. She had expected her mother to round on her, to call her ungrateful. 'What do you mean?'

'I know it isn't the same as the whole bolt of cloth – the way it shines as it falls, that's what makes it so striking – but I could make you a bodice, Colette. Or – or a cap. Or I could dress one of the dolls in it.' Her mother laughed sadly. 'You loved those dolls so much when you were little. I used to have to wrench them out of your hands to show the customers.'

'Did you?' Colette didn't remember. 'Was that – a long time ago?'

Her mother's face closed over – as if she was waiting for what Colette would say next. But Colette only smiled at her, and kissed her cheek, and went to climb the little winding staircase up to her room.

She knew Ma would never tell her what she wanted to know.

Colette had first asked where her father was when she was very small – other children seemed to have one, though not all of them, by any means. She had been curious. Ma had explained that he was dead. He had died of a fever, shortly after Colette was born. Having never known him, Colette hadn't felt this to be too much of a loss. She supposed that if she had had a father, Ma might not have had to work so hard – and she might not have had to start her own training as a seamstress so early. But then every other child she knew helped in their parents' shop, or workroom. Even the little daughters of the nobility who came to be measured for their dresses had lessons, it seemed, in deportment and dancing and languages. Colette thought she would prefer to sit by her window and sew.

What was strange was that Ma wouldn't ever tell her any more about her father. Did Colette look like him? Did he have hair that curled too? Had he been able to sing? Was that where her own soft, pretty voice had come from, since Ma herself said she croaked like a heron? Had he been a tailor? A boatman? A maker of wigs?

'He's dead, Colette. Dead and gone and best forgotten.' That was all Ma would say. Colette had asked so many times and she always said the same. But hearing the words over and over again made them sound less like truth, not more. Over the years, as her mother grew more agitated each time he was mentioned, and more determined not to tell Colette anything, Colette had become convinced that there was some dark, hidden secret about her father.

She would stare at her face in the dark surface of

the canal, cursing as the wind ruffled the water. There was a glass in the showroom, of course, but it was old and mottled, and Ma would see what she was doing and know what she meant by it. The water was just as good, when it held still. She leaned over her reflection, staring at her face and trying to subtract those features that she recognised from her mother, to see what was left. Curling reddish fair hair, and hazel eyes, and perhaps the determined point of her chin?

Colette curled up on the bed she shared with her mother, tugging the blankets up around her shoulders. As she fell asleep, her father's voice whispered to her in the faint hissing of the night wind on the water.

'It's beautiful, Colette,' Ma murmured, turning the fabric this way and that to look at the dancing golden fish. Colette had used a scrap of old blue cambric, a fine cotton, as they couldn't waste the precious silk for samples. Even so, the fish glittered in the dim light of the workroom, as if they would leap away from the faded material and make for the canal outside the door.

'Good enough to show to Madame the Countess?'

Ma nodded, smiling, and Colette sat back, twitching her shoulders gratefully – she had been hunched over her embroidery ever since she'd got up that morning. She had crept out of bed at first light, hoping to leave Ma to sleep – who knows how late she'd stayed up the night before, cutting out the pieces of the blue silk, and tacking them together. There had been no time to make a toile out of calico as the countess was in too much of a hurry for her grand ball dress. The dress was on the wicker mannequin now, looming in the corner of the room. But Ma had come trailing down the stairs not long after her, to finish twitching and fussing with the deep folds of silk that draped down the back of the dress.

Now, she heated a pan of coffee over the kitchen fire. They had crumbly, dry biscuits to dip in it, and Colette wondered if the countess would have biscuits too. Her maid would bring them to her in bed, a huge pile of them, with an eggshell-thin porcelain bowl of sweet chocolate. She would be wearing that lace-trimmed wrapper with the pink ribbons that Ma had made for her. Colette sighed, and licked the crumbs off her fingers enviously. She didn't envy the clothes, or not all that much. But if no one had ordered a dress, she and Ma made do with the bread that the baker sold off at the end of the day.

Carefully, they carried the wicker form out into the showroom, turning it this way and that, so as to catch the sunlight on the gleaming silk. Colette pinned her embroidered fish over the plain calico toile they'd made for the underskirt, and Ma sat limply in the delicate chair they kept for clients, staring at the dress. There was other work to be done – simpler dresses for less important clients – but neither of them had the energy to hurry back to the workroom. It was not the time to start on fashioning an outdated striped woollen robe into something more up to date for the grain merchant's wife. It felt like too much of a comedown after the blue silk.

The countess arrived later that morning, disembarking from her gilded gondola in a flurry of servants and onlookers.

'Is she really very rich?' Colette asked, watching a group of women and children staring and curtseying as the countess stalked by. Their neighbour, Alyssa, caught her eye, and nodded to her encouragingly. A rich customer was good for all of them – if Colette and Ma had money, they'd have a little food to spare, perhaps, and maybe even some scraps of pretty fabric to make dresses for the children. 'She's part of the court, isn't she? I'm surprised she doesn't have her dresses made somewhere more fashionable. She must have the money to spend.' She pursed her lips as the countess's page boy flung a few small coins at the watchers, and the children scrambled and fought for the pennies.

Ma shrugged. 'Who knows, Colette? Perhaps her family's vineyards have failed, or they've mortgaged away the estates? Or perhaps she just has a nose for a bargain. We don't ask questions. She's our only court client, and we must keep her happy.'

'Is it ready?' the countess demanded, as she edged her way impatiently through the door, followed by her page and the maid. She had on the busy patterned silk again, and it made Colette's teeth ache. It was open over a different petticoat this time, in a shade of pink that swore at the embroidery. But there were rose-pink pearls all along the petticoat hem, and in and out of the silver flowers on the stiff stomacher she wore – the dress might be horrible, but it screamed of money. She had a mask on too, a half-mask of pink, stiffened silk, tied with trailing ribbons. It made her eyes glitter, and Colette wasn't sure if that was just the effect of the pink silk, or if the mask was spelled to make the countess look more beautiful.

'Yes, my lady,' Ma murmured, moving aside the painted screen they'd put in front of the dress. As she pulled it away, the sun caught the silk in a blaze of blue light, and the countess's maid, Sofie, stepped back with a gasp. Even the countess's mouth fell open, though she didn't make a sound. She cast the maid a disgusted look, then slowly paced around the dress, examining the cut of the sleeves.

'To be worn over a shift with deep lace cuffs, my lady,' Ma murmured. 'We could supply the lace, of course.' There was a hopeful gleam in her eyes.

'Mmmm.' The countess inclined her head slowly. 'I will try it.' She stood expectantly, waiting for Ma to bow her into the tiny dressing room behind the curtains. Colette whisked the dress from the mannequin, and then waited outside, poised, ready to fetch pins, or scissors, or whatever Ma called for. Sofie sank wearily onto one of the chairs, and glared at Colette as if daring her to comment. From behind the curtain there was a low rustling of silk, interspersed with irritable grunts from the countess as the dress was tugged and laced and pinned into place.

Colette paced, biting at the skin on the side of her thumbnail. The dress had to be perfect, but a tiny part of her still hoped the countess would tear it off and leave the silk behind for them to keep. The leftover pieces were tucked lovingly in an old wooden press, scented with lavender and dried rose petals, waiting for Ma to have a spare moment to fashion something for Colette, but the dress itself still called to her.

She could almost hear the threads whispering – the silk spoke to her as it rustled across the wooden boards, and the countess emerged from behind the curtain.

'My lady,' the countess's maid sighed, clasping her hands. Colette thought she would have said her mistress looked beautiful whatever the dress had been like – but that sigh of delight had been an honest one. 'Oh, indeed, Madame is a picture.'

The countess shook out the skirts of the overdress, and patted the silk. She swayed from side to side, and paced a few steps, all the while eyeing herself in the mirror. 'You really should have a better glass,' she complained, peering over her shoulder at the long falls of silk down the back of the gown. 'This one is pitiful…'

'I know, my lady,' Ma agreed, twisting her fingers. 'But mirrors are so expensive. Are you happy with the embroidery, my lady? The little fishes?'

Colette glanced down at her work – the countess had kept her pale pink stomacher and petticoat on, but Ma had tucked the embroidered piece under the open front of the dress. Colette smiled to herself as she watched the fish sparkling – they looked as if they were moving, their tiny fins flickering to and fro.

Then her throat seemed to close, and her heart thudded painfully in her chest. They *were* moving. They swirled their tails lazily against the limp blue cambric – except that now the cambric had the same rich, blue-green tint of the silk, and rippled like waves.

Colette fought for breath. It was happening again. Her very best work seemed to move sometimes, but never so clearly as this. She had always convinced herself that she was imagining it, before, but this time she was certain it was real.

No one else could see it – or they hadn't noticed.

Ma was politely haggling with the countess about the first payment for the dress, explaining that she needed the money to pay for the silk. Sofie and the page boy were yawning in the corner. Colette clasped her hands tightly behind her back. She wanted to touch the fish, to stroke the fabric and see if it was watery. Her fingers were twitching. But she couldn't, of course.

The fish twirled and looped and fluttered their tails, and Colette gazed at them hungrily, wondering how it had happened. What had she done to make the stitches move? *It has to be something about the silk*, she thought vaguely. It had swallowed up that sea water. Perhaps it had taken in some of the city's water magic, and bound it up with its own strange powers from the East? There were many deep magics practised there, Colette was sure, somewhere so strange and different from Venice.

The whispering of the silk filled Colette's ears again, and she glanced anxiously at the overdress – what if the countess heard? But she was too busy peacocking in front of the mirror, admiring the curve of her arms in the elbow sleeves and interrogating Ma about the cost of trimmings.

It wasn't only the whispering, Colette saw, digging her fingernails into her palms. There were pictures. Strange little images fluttered across the fabric: Colette's tiny golden fish sparkled and glittered and swam onto the skirts of the dress, then they turned into coins, a cascade of gold pieces that were swallowed up into the darkness of the silk. And then – Ma! Colette stifled a gasp. Her mother shimmered on the surface of the fabric, shaking like Colette's own reflection had in the dark waters of the canal. She was snatching at the coins, but they slipped out of her fingers, again and again, and then she pressed her hands against her face, and faded away.

'I will send Sofie with the money,' the countess said, waving a hand vaguely, as if money was something with which she did not concern herself. 'Soon…'

No, you won't… Colette thought grimly. She was

sure the pictures on the silk were right – the countess was intending to cheat them somehow. The dress was reflecting her darkest thoughts. She wondered if anyone else would be able to see them – did the silk speak to her alone? Because she loved it? Because she had spent so long with it in her arms?

She reached out at last, pretending to straighten the pleats across the countess's shoulders. She had to touch the fabric.

Colette felt the magic like a delicious coolness as her fingers brushed over the surface, a coolness that shivered over her skin and made her smile. Then the smile faded as the countess turned to stare at her, and so did Ma, and the magic settled inside her as a ball of ice, a premonition of something dreadful that was coming, all too soon.

'But what were you doing?' Ma asked again. 'I can't understand it, Colette. You know what an important customer she is! And now she thinks you're touched, or rag-mannered at best. What were you doing, standing there staring at her like that? You know we can't risk offending her.'

'I know,' Colette muttered dully. The silk was stretched out over her lap – now that the countess had approved the pattern, she could start stitching the thousands of tiny fish that would dart over the dress.

'Honestly, Colette! You must have had a reason.'

Colette hung her head over the icy smoothness of the silk, remembering that cold foretelling. She could hear Ma breathing beside her, each breath ending in the faintest rattle. 'It's this silk!' she whispered at last. 'It's strange. There were pictures in it…'

'Pictures? Don't talk nonsense.'

Colette sighed faintly. Ma didn't trust magic – even in a city like Venice, which was practically built on it. She muttered the old sewing spells in a gabble, and more out of habit than anything else. 'You said yourself there was something special about it,' she pointed out.

'But not magic. We don't have anything to do with

real *magic*. Only those old rhymes, that's all. Proper work, that's what goes into our dresses. No silly, flighty spells.'

'Well, this dress has got something in it,' Colette muttered. 'And I pity the countess when she's wearing it, Ma, because I don't think it likes her.'

'Don't say things like that!' Ma's voice rose into a hoarse shriek, and she coughed painfully, her sides heaving. 'Honestly, Colette, never! She'll have us up before the law. Don't you dare.'

'I didn't do anything!' Colette wailed. 'It's in the silk!'

'Oh, I've no patience with you!' Ma turned away, settling back in her chair and snatching up the bodice she was seaming. Colette looked over at her miserably. Ma wouldn't understand – she didn't want to. Colette didn't see why her mother was so dismissive of magic. She seemed to hate it, almost. Colette set a few more stitches, and then leaned against the window, cooling her burning face against the greenish glass. The street outside was busy, and she watched the passers-by, wishing for once that she could be out there on the *calle* with them. She loved to sew, and she felt herself lucky, working as an apprentice in her own mother's workshop, instead of slaving for a stranger. But today the atmosphere in the sewing room was close and angry, and Colette longed to hurry away and lose herself among the crowd, just for a little while.

There was no time, of course. Two more weeks until the dress was to be finished. The countess had sent out invitations to her grand evening party – all of Venice's nobility had been invited. The dress must be finished, or Ma's business would be ruined. Colette sat up straighter, and sewed two more tiny fish. Then she straightened the fabric, to check that she hadn't puckered it with her stitches, and the fish fluttered over her fingers in a chilly wisp. She shivered, and pushed it away a little, leaning back against the window.

There was a girl strolling by, not a common shop-girl like Colette, but not a noblewoman, either. A merchant's daughter, Colette decided, with a practised look at her dress and cloak. Colette glanced up at the girl's face and flinched. She had on a mute mask – a black velvet mask that covered the central part of her face, even her mouth. It had no strings to tie it on – the girl was holding on it with her teeth, biting on a button on the back of the mask, so she couldn't open her mouth. Only her eyes shone through the choking velvet, gleaming pale blue against the darkness of the mask. It made Colette shudder just to look at her. How could she wear such a thing? Colette could only suppose that her family made her, so that when she went out into the city there was no chance of her speaking to anyone she shouldn't.

Masks were everywhere in Venice, but Colette had never liked them. She had seen her ma in one, just once, a thin golden mask that, looking back, Colette realised must have been quite valuable. It was some sort of fabric, perhaps even lace, and it had been cobweb-thin, and glittery. It had hung on the wall in the workroom, gathering dust, until one year's carnival, when Alyssa and some of the other neighbour women had persuaded Colette's ma out to join a late-night dance along the canal. Ma had shaken her head at first, and said she was too busy, but they'd begged and wheedled, and in the end she had laughed, and snatched the mask down from the wall. Colette had watched from the stairs, wide-eyed, as the gold ribbons seemed to tie themselves behind her head, and she had begun to dance. Just one foot tapping, to start with, but then the other, and her fingers fluttering as she glided to the door.

She had glanced back once, as the door swung shut behind her. Colette could see the eyes glittering behind the golden lace, but they were not her mother's. She had crept back up the stairs weeping, and hidden herself under the blankets. In the morning her mother had been back, and Colette had watched her cautiously for the whole day. She was the same as she ever had been, but the mask had disappeared. She had never dared to ask where it had gone. She hadn't wanted to know.

Since then, even the plainest papier-mâché half-mask had made Colette suspicious. *Why not just wear your own face?* she always wondered. *What are you hiding?* There were a few places in the city where masks were compulsory – some of the votes for elected officials were held masked, to make the ballot truly secret. *Because no one would dare admit who they had voted for*, Colette thought sadly, *in case the losing candidate decided to pay them a visit.*

All the partygoers at the Ridotto, the largest and most luxurious of the casinos, went masked too. Duchess Olivia, the ruler of the city, had let it be known that she disapproved of the dangerous habit of gambling. Especially after so many of the young men from her court had devastated their family's fortunes in the Ridotto's shadowy gaming rooms. So now the nobility slunk through its doors cloaked and masked, and the sense of danger and intrigue and forbidden excitement had made the place busier than ever.

As the masked girl passed closer to the window,

Colette saw her eyes flick sideways – to Colette's own face, pressed against the glass, pale and horrified. The mask shifted a little, and the girl bent her head down and hurried away. Colette could just see a faint, silvery-green haze floating around the fussy, mouse-brown ringlets of her hair. The mask was enchanted, then. Why didn't they just lock her up in the house? Colette cursed quietly to herself as she jabbed the embroidery needle into her finger.

'Don't watch.' Colette hadn't seen her mother coming up beside her, she had been so intent on the masked girl on the other side of the window. 'Did you hurt yourself?'

'Just pricked my finger. It's nothing,' Colette told her dismally. 'Did you see that girl?'

'Yes.' Her mother's voice was so low Colette could hardly hear her. 'Poor little thing. She isn't the first I've seen in one of those, either. I shouldn't have shouted at you, Colette. Did you really see that, in the silk? You mean it?'

'Yes. I promise. I didn't make it up. And Ma – that

girl that just walked past, there was a spell on her mask. I could see it. It was all greenish.' She didn't mention the way the golden fish had moved again. What if she had done that, somehow? In spite of her mother's suspicion of spells – the way she had always been taught that magic was untrustworthy, dangerous and frankly bad – a shiver of excitement ran over Colette's skin. This was something new. Something different. A small joy, to lift her, just a little, out of the workroom, and the seams and the embroidery and the callused fingers. She had expected this life would be hers for ever – she was a seamstress, and happy to be. But still... Just a little magic...

Colette's mother laid a hand on her shoulder. 'I should have known,' she murmured faintly. She broke into another fit of coughing, so violent that she could hardly stand. Colette sprang up, holding her, feeling the pain of the spasms shaking her mother's body, and trying not to cry. This was what happened when she forgot her place, and started her silly dreaming. But what had Ma meant, *I should have known?*

Ma sank into her chair, pressing a handkerchief against her lips, eyes closed.

'You're getting worse,' Colette said flatly. She had pretended for so long that it was a matter of the right food, fresher air, or just getting the winter damp out of Ma's bones. But as her mother leaned back in her chair and let the handkerchief flutter out of her fingers, Colette saw that it was darkened with spots of blood.

Chapter Three

COLETTE STOOD BY THE WATER, staring at the patterns that the evening sunlight threw onto the ripples. She had persuaded Ma to go and lie down for a while, and then she had stitched away at the golden fish until her fingers were so cramped she could no longer force the needle through the fabric. She had listened at the foot of the stairs, but Ma seemed to have gone to sleep, so she slipped out, thinking she'd walk a little by the canal, and perhaps buy a hot meat pie to take home for supper.

A faint thread of sound floated down the canal towards her, and Colette blinked, confused. Music – and not just a boatman singing to himself as he poled his craft home, either. It sounded like a full band – strings, flutes, all anchored by the beat of a drum. Colette peered through the gathering shadows, trying to see what was coming down the canal. Then she caught her breath, stepping back and dropping into a curtsey. She recognised the barge – every Venetian would. No matter how busy they were with work, she and Ma turned out for all the festivals: the Wedding of the Sea, the Blessing of the Waters, the new thanksgiving ceremony for the Leviathan's Leaving just two years before. The grand, gilded craft slipping down the canal towards her was Duchess Olivia's personal barge, the smaller craft, the one that carried the duchess and her attendants out to the huge, sea-going vessel that made the journey into the lagoon. And the duchess must be on it, surely, for why else would the band be playing?

The barge ploughed towards her, and Colette lifted

her head, just a little – enough to catch a glimpse of the duchess, and maybe even her cousin, the Lady Mia. She had been the one, so the stories went, the mage who had calmed the waters when the great form of the Leviathan had risen up from the sea bed and flooded the city.

Two pale horses swam past her, almost close enough to touch, and Colette forgot her curtsey, jumping up to smile at them in delight. She had never seen any of the water horses so close. Ma did not like her to swim, and Colette had never been one of the children who played with the horses in the water in front of the palace. The smaller horse veered closer, and gazed at Colette with huge dark eyes. 'Good evening, child,' she murmured, sweet-voiced.

'Good evening, my lady.' Hastily, Colette curtseyed again. The horses were part of the duchess's court; it was quite proper to address this one as if she were some high-ranking noble. But Colette would have said 'my lady' even if that weren't so, as the silver-white horse was so beautiful.

'You look sad,' the horse murmured, leaning closer, and Colette swallowed hard, feeling tears spring behind her eyes.

'I – I suppose,' Colette agreed haltingly.

The horse came closer, nudging at Colette with her soft pinkish muzzle. 'You'll grow into your magic soon, dear one. You should be glad.'

Colette stared at her. 'How…how did you know?'

The silvery creature snorted, and nudged her again. A lock of her mane coiled itself around Colette's shoulders, full of warmth and love and a feeling of joy that seemed to shimmer all over Colette, like a shower of cool water. 'It's inside you. Bubbling away under your skin, just waiting. Remember – don't be afraid.'

'I won't… I mean, I'll try…' Colette whispered, as the barge drew alongside them, and the horse slipped back to swim alongside it again. She saw two girls a few years older than herself staring down from the side, and swallowed hard, remembering to curtsey again. The younger girl waved at her, smiling, and the older one nodded regally, and then her face broke into a smile too.

Colette gulped, remembering that she shouldn't stare – she couldn't help it. Neither of them was beautiful – not any more beautiful than most girls. But there was something that made it impossible for her to look away. *It must be the magic*, she thought, her fingers clenching on the fabric of her skirts. *And I have it too – I* do *have it, the water horse said so, and Ma…* She shivered for a moment, remembering the blood on Ma's handkerchief. Then she squashed the image of those red spots away. Couldn't she be a little selfish, just for once? *I could be like them, just a little.* She gazed after the barge as it moved slowly down the canal, staring until it had slipped away into the darkness, and she could no longer hear the music. Then she wondered back to the shop, dreaming…

She heard the coughing as she came out of the little passageway and onto their *calle*. It echoed out of their poorly fitting upstairs window, a hard, painful sound that seemed to go on and on. Colette flinched, all her happy imaginings flittering away like the dreams they were. What did pretty horses and princesses and magic matter, when Ma was— She wasn't going to say it.

Colette clenched her fists, her nails almost cutting into her skin, listening as the coughs died away into harsh, rattling breaths. 'What am I going to do?' she whispered to the tortoiseshell cat. It was there again, sitting on the end of the balustrade, staring at her with wide, golden eyes.

'You know, I wouldn't mind if you did answer, after all,' Colette said, cautiously rubbing the cat behind the ears. 'I didn't want you to before, but I've no one else to talk to. And I'm sure you know what I'm saying. You have that look about you. Like that silver horse did.' Then she sighed. 'I didn't even mention Ma to her, you know. She could see I was sad, and she thought it was because I'm scared of the strange things that keep happening. And I am, it's just that there are worse things to be frightened of.' She looked the cat in the eyes. 'You're very good at listening, cat. Couldn't you tell me something useful?

Perhaps all cats have that look. Perhaps I'm just desperate for anyone to tell me what I can do about… about Ma.' Her voice dropped into a strangled sort of whisper, and she leaned closer to the cat, breathing into its ragged ear. 'I don't think she's going to get better, cat. There was blood on her handkerchief. It's the consumption, I know it is. She's coughing up her lungs.'

The cat nudged her. Just the merest touch with the firm, warm top of its head against her chin. Colette gulped, the breath catching in her throat. After a moment she went on more steadily. 'There isn't a cure, you know. Even the richest people don't get better. They just die slower, because they've got servants to fuss over them, and nicer things to eat.' She swallowed. What she wanted to say next sounded heartless, but she couldn't help it. 'What will happen to me, cat? When she's gone? What does the magic even matter, if I haven't a home?'

'Colette…' A faint whisper echoed across the empty *calle*, and Colette whirled around. The cat leaped away and disappeared across the bridge. The faint whispering sounded so eerie that for a moment Colette thought it was the strange magic in the silk calling to her again. Or even the voice she had heard in her dreams, the voice she had somehow known was her father.

But it was only Ma, leaning against the door of the shop, her face frighteningly white.

'I just had to get some air,' Colette told her guiltily, running back to the shop.

Ma put an arm around her, and Colette could feel the fever in her, burning her up from the inside. 'You're working too hard,' Ma murmured, and Colette gasped in surprised laughter.

'Me!'

Ma sighed and patted her cheek. 'I know. But the dress is nearly finished. A day or so more sewing, and then I can help you with the embroidery.' She stepped back, holding Colette by the shoulders and gazing at her. 'And then I shall make you something, Colette. I'm sure there's enough silk left for a pretty bodice.'

Colette nodded. She wasn't sure she would ever wear whatever Ma made. When would she have an occasion to wear a blue silk bodice? And wouldn't it look odd over her plain linen shifts and woollen skirts? Even if she did find something to wear with it, Colette wasn't sure she wanted to wear that blue silk. There was something in it that called to her, something dangerous, but so enticing.

Colette shifted lazily, and pulled the blanket higher up around her ears. There was a shaft of sunlight striking through the small window, and their attic room seemed full of golden light. She sat up suddenly, still only half-awake and blinking in the light. Something was wrong – she couldn't work out what. She stared around uncertainly, and ran her fingers through her hair. The light. This was no clear early morning brightness. They had overslept. It was hardly surprising, though – she and Ma had finished the dress the night before, leaving them a day for the last fittings and alterations for Madame the

Countess. It had been long past midnight when the last tiny golden fish swam out into the silk – and by then Colette couldn't tell whether it was weariness or magic that made her embroidery move.

'Ma…' she whispered gently. 'Shall I go down and heat us up some coffee? The countess is coming this morning, we've slept in. I could even fetch us a honey cake from the pastry cook, to celebrate. After all, the countess will have to pay you soon, won't she?' Colette squashed down the sickening pictures she had seen reflected in the silk. The countess couldn't refuse to pay for the dress. Ma could report her to the Guild; their lawyers would force her to give them the gold, surely? Or they could quietly suggest that it wouldn't be good for the countess's reputation if she was known to be short of money…

'Ma…' Colette leaned over to look at her, and sighed. She was still so deeply asleep – she hadn't even murmured. 'Ma, the countess will be coming for the fitting. We need to take the dress through to the showroom.'

Colette's thoughts were settling in her head so slowly, like spoon-marks in syrup. She was still too dazed with sleep to think straight. Now that she had worked out that they'd overslept, that awful sense of something wrong should have gone. It hadn't. *The room is too quiet*, she decided anxiously, gazing down at Ma. There were faint cries from the larger canal a few streets away, the boatmen calling to each other. A bird was twittering on the roof beyond the window. But that was all. The only sound in the attic room was Colette's own breathing. And it was speeding up, growing more shallow, as though her body had worked out that something was very wrong, even if she hadn't.

Ma was not breathing. There was no sound from her at all.

'Ma!' Colette grabbed her shoulders and shook her, and Ma's head slipped a little to one side. A tiny trickle of blood-stained foam showed at the corner of her mouth, angrily red against the pallor of her skin.

'No!' Colette whispered, catching Ma's face in her

hands, patting insistently at her cheeks. 'Ma, no!' But she could feel the slack weight of her mother's head, pressing against her hands. There was nothing there, nothing of Ma left.

'You finished the dress,' Colette murmured, letting go. 'You finished the dress for that – that woman first. And then you died. All neat and tidy. Oh, Ma!'

She crawled over to the other side of the bed, as far away from the body as she could, and pressed her hand into her mouth to stop herself from howling. She couldn't scream and cry, not now, however much she wanted to. The rent was due. There was a dress to fit – a dress made of a fabric laced with God-knows-what magic. Magic that seemed to show itself to her alone.

Colette was ten years old, and she had no one.

'Where is your mother?' The countess eyed Colette haughtily as the girl dropped into a curtsey.

Colette gulped. 'She was…called away, my lady.' She couldn't tell the countess Ma was dead. She still hadn't worked out what she was going to do. She had to tell someone what had happened, but she didn't know who, and the countess and her entourage had arrived before she could decide. She had straightened out the bedclothes, and folded Ma's hands across her chest, but that was all.

Besides, if she told the countess what had happened, she might well decide not to take the dress, in case it was tainted with Ma's consumption. 'A sick relative, my lady. Ma had to go to her. But I can make the last alterations, I promise you.'

The countess inclined her head ungraciously. 'Oh, very well. I have no time to wait for your mother. After all, my ball is tomorrow. It's most inconsiderate of your mother not to be here.'

Colette choked down an angry retort. 'She would rather be here, too, my lady…' she whispered, as she helped the countess into the blue silk dress, and started to pin in the embroidered stomacher. Her fingers slipped and stuttered, and she pricked herself with one of the pins. But she hardly felt it – it didn't seem to matter. And the drop of blood disappeared away into the fabric, just as the salt water had.

'Good. Yes, very good.' The countess turned slowly in front of the mirror, inspecting the fine details of the embroidery. 'It will be perfect for tomorrow.' She looked thoughtfully at Colette. 'You *have* inherited your mother's skills,' she commented. 'You are apprenticed to her by the Guild, I suppose?'

'Yes,' Colette whispered, as she and the maidservant, Sofie, helped the countess back into her old dress. 'Yes, I am.' *No. I don't know what I am any more. An orphan, I suppose.* She swallowed down panic. The Tailors' Guild had an orphanage, for children whose parents had paid their Guild dues until their death. She had forgotten. That would be where she would have to go. She had seen the orphans before, walking to church on Sundays, in neat brown dresses, and brown knickerbocker suits for the boys. They were silent, and the street had hushed as they passed, only to break out into murmurs of sympathy once the little line had turned the corner. She would be one of those pitiable little girls in brown.

'Tell your mother to come to me at the palazzo for her payment.' The countess waved a hand dismissively, as if money was something she did think about.

'But, my lady—' Colette began, starting forward.

'What?' The countess stared down her nose.

'I thought – my mother thought, that is – that you would pay her today. She said you would.'

'I can hardly leave the payment with a child.' The countess sniffed. 'Don't be ridiculous. She can come to the palazzo. In a few days. I shall be too busy tomorrow, of course, and then I shall be exhausted after the ball. Yes, in a few days.'

We don't have a few days, Colette wanted to wail. *Ma doesn't have any time at all, and I don't know what to do. If I don't have the money, what happens about a funeral?*

But the countess had gone, tap-tapping away in her neat heels over the stones. Colette stood in the doorway, staring after the black and gilt gondola, tears streaking down her face.

'Little Colette! Whatever's the matter?' Their neighbour Alyssa stopped to peer at her, and smoothed away a tear with her thumb. 'Was it the countess? Your mother's told me about her. A good thing to have a rich customer, of course, but they keep you running after them like lapdogs. Did she say something to you, is that it?'

Colette shook her head. 'She won't pay,' she whispered. 'And I need the money for the funeral.'

Alyssa dropped her basket. 'Funeral? Colette, what's happened? Not your ma? Oh, Colette. When?'

'She was dead when I woke up this morning. I don't know what to do, Alyssa. She's still there.'

'You poor child. Here!' She turned to a couple of little boys, kicking a stone along the edge of the canal. 'Run to the church and call Father Stephano. Tell him he must come at once to Madame Harriet's.' She turned back to the small girl in front of her. 'Old Anna and I will lay your ma out, Colette, we'd be glad to, with all the mending she's done for us, and the fabric scraps she's passed on.'

Colette nodded dumbly. She had nothing to say – it was as though now Alyssa knew, everything was moving too fast. She had been swept up in a tide, and it would not let her go until she was left at the Guild orphanage, in one of those faded brown dresses.

'So this is the child?'

'Yes, Father.' Alyssa ducked her head respectfully. 'Her mother was a good churchgoer, Father, when she could. She brought little Colette with her. Didn't she, Colette?'

'Yes, Father.' Colette wasn't sure that Ma would have wanted the old priest to officiate at her funeral – she hadn't much liked him; she said he lived off the poor, always after gifts or a meal. And there was certainly not enough money for a grand funeral, or a headstone, or even a tiny plaque in the wall of the church. Or not until Colette had found some way of getting the money out of the countess. Perhaps the priest wouldn't want such a sad little ceremony in his grand church. But there had to be something – some way of ending things. 'Can she be buried in the church?' she pleaded. 'I haven't any money, but we're owed some. Can I pay later?'

The old priest sighed and tutted, and nodded his head. 'I will enquire with the Guild,' he murmured, quite kindly. 'She may have paid into the burial fund. And then of course…' He eyed Colette, and added in a doleful whisper. 'There is the orphanage.'

'Oh…' Alyssa gave Colette a troubled look. 'Must she go there, Father? Isn't there any other way? It seems so hard, for Colette to have to leave. Perhaps I could keep her?'

Colette looked up at her neighbour, surprised and delighted. Alyssa had been one of her mother's only friends, but she certainly hadn't expected Alyssa to give her a home.

'No, no, no. That would not be right at all. She belongs with the Guild, as is proper. She must be educated to follow in her mother's footsteps,' said the old priest sternly. 'The Guild orphanage is undoubtedly the place. I shall speak to the trustees.'

Alyssa nodded humbly. She regarded the priest's word as law, Colette could see.

'Thank you,' Colette whispered in Alyssa's ear. 'I won't forget.'

The tide rolled on, just as Colette had known it would, sweeping her along with it. She'd slept since that first night on a pile of old calico toiles in the workroom – Alyssa and Anna, another of their neighbours, had washed her mother's body, and dressed her in her Sunday clothes, leaving her lying on the bed until the next morning, and the burial. Colette had hardly gone upstairs in the few days since – she had stayed sewing in the workroom, hurrying up the rickety staircase to snatch a little bread out of the kitchen, and a clean chemise from the press in the corner of the bedroom. She hadn't looked at the bed.

The priest had gone to the orphanage, she knew. They'd come for her, sooner or later. Would it make the slightest difference, if she said she didn't want to go? *If only I could have got that money from the countess,*

Colette thought bitterly, a tear dropping on her stitches. *Then I could have paid the rent.* But even then, she suspected, the priest and the Guildmasters might have said she was too young to live alone. Since her mother had paid Guild dues, they owed Colette charity – even if she didn't want it.

Colette brushed the tears away hurriedly as the shop door banged, and Alyssa came hurrying through into the workroom, a worried look on her thin face.

'They're here, Colette – Father Stephano, and this old pair from the Guild orphanage.' She gazed at Colette helplessly, as heavy footsteps came clumping after her. 'Oh, my little dear… I'll take them upstairs, boil some coffee. Tidy your hair, Colette.'

Colette nodded, and swallowed the bitter taste in her throat. Her hands smoothed automatically over her hair, but she knew the red-gold flyaway curls would look untidy however she tried to pin them down.

She brushed the threads from her skirts, and looked sadly at her worn-down slippers. If only she looked neater. More – more loved. *But I have been loved*, she thought fiercely. It was only that she was growing, and they hadn't had the money for new shoes just yet. Grimly, she marched up the stairs towards their living quarters, and the sharp voices she could hear in the kitchen. She peered around the edge of the door, watching as Alyssa argued with the priest and the two strangers.

The stout woman from the orphanage looked around the little kitchen, and sniffed dismissively. 'The sooner she is out of this place the better,' she murmured to the priest. Father Stephano nodded, and then added apologetically, 'But I do believe the mother to have been of good character.'

'She certainly was!' Alyssa snapped indignantly, glaring at the stout woman, and the thin, elderly man in dusty black who had come with her from the Guild orphanage. 'Excuse me, Father, but I don't know what these people, these *trustees* – I don't know what they're thinking, with poor Harriet not cold in her grave! She was a most respectable dressmaker, with several clients in the nobility. And her house always kept beautifully clean.'

'It is a most irregular situation.' The stout woman sniffed again. 'A female, setting up in the tailoring business. A foreigner and not married.'

'She was married. My father is dead,' Colette put in. It was the first time she had spoken, and they all stared at her, as though they were rather surprised that she could.

'That's as may be,' muttered the stout woman, and Colette frowned. Surely it was quite respectable to be a widow? Did she think that Ma ought to have looked after her husband better?

'The woman's goods and chattels had better be sold,' the dusty gentleman pronounced. 'I gather there is rent owing. Of course.'

'Only because the countess hasn't paid!' Colette cried. They were making it sound as though Ma hadn't looked after her properly. 'She ordered a dress for a grand party she was giving, and Ma finished it the night before she died. She said to go and call for the payment at the Palazzo Morezzi. The countess's payment will pay the rent, I promise you.'

The man's old, creased face sharpened, the eyes glittering amongst the folds of skin. 'Countess Morezzi? That money will belong to the Guild,' he snapped. 'It will be used to pay for the child's care and education.' His hands twisted amongst the yellowed lace ruffles at his wrists, and Colette shivered.

'I – that is, the church – must be paid for the funeral,' the priest put in quickly.

'There will be a certain amount,' the old man admitted, sounding quite reluctant. 'Madame Harriet had made an arrangement with the Guild. So there is no claim on the remainder of the money.'

'Shabby old vulture,' Alyssa muttered to herself unhappily. But then she caught Colette's eye and smiled, although her smile wasn't very convincing. 'Don't worry, little dear,' she whispered. 'I'll come and visit you.'

'No visitors,' snapped the stout woman.

'Why ever not?' Alyssa put her arm around Colette,

hugging her tightly. Colette felt a thickness in her throat and bit her bottom lip, not wanting to cry in front of the trustees.

'Orphans don't have visitors.' The stout woman shook her head disapprovingly, as if the very idea were improper.

A thin, tinkling noise sounded in the kitchen, and Colette jumped, pulling away from Alyssa. 'The shop – that's the bell in the shop. I have to go.' She darted past the old man, who tried to grab her sleeve, and down the stairs to the shop, where the countess's page boy was standing with the bell. The countess herself was outside in the *calle*, huddled against the wind in a fur-lined cloak, and looking deeply irritable.

'My lady!'

'Is it true, what I have heard?' she snapped. 'Your mother is dead?'

'Yes,' Colette faltered.

'You lied to me. You said she had been called away.'

'She died that night, my lady.' Colette spoke to the

countess's shoes. There were little jewels stitched onto the toes: a flower made out of purple stones. 'I found her in the morning. And then I heard you arriving. I wasn't sure what to say.'

'She was dead, upstairs, while you were fitting my dress?' the countess demanded incredulously.

'Yes,' Colette whispered.

There was a flurry in the doorway of the shop, and the trustees, the priest and Alyssa spilled out onto the *calle*, and stared at the countess. The old man bowed hurriedly, and the priest tried to nod his head in a dignified way, then gave up and bowed too. Alyssa ducked back into the doorway, but the stout woman curtseyed very low, and turned scarlet as her stays creaked.

'Who are these?' the countess demanded of Colette, drawing one hand from her fur muff to wave at them.

'The priest from the church where my mother was buried two days past,' Colette explained. 'And these are the trustees of the orphanage. The Tailors' Guild orphanage. I have to go to it.' She folded her lips together tightly, pressing back an awful desire to laugh. It was the very worst time – how could she want to? But the countess sounded as if she was talking about cockroaches creeping out of her bedroom walls. The tortoiseshell cat was sitting on the pillar at the end of the bridge again, she noticed. It seemed to be watching the little scene – it was absolutely still, in the way of cats. Colette sobered herself, and it seemed to look at her approvingly.

The countess stared at her for a moment. Then she shook her head decisively. 'No.'

'My lady, I don't think you understand,' the old man began, his voice rather muffled, since he was bowing again. 'The child's mother was a member of our Guild. The child herself is an apprentice, despite her young age. We will take her into the orphanage for the moment, and look for a household to send her to, as an apprentice.'

'No,' the countess repeated. 'I will take her. Fetch your things, girl.'

Colette merely gaped at her, but the old man shot upright. 'My lady… This is… This is…'

'This is nothing to do with you,' the countess pronounced.

'Forgive me, my lady, but the Guild—'

'You may tell the Guild that I have employed the child as a sewing maid. She will be most carefully provided for. Is that not what you want?'

The old man gobbled as he tried to find some reason to deny the countess, and keep Colette and her money. Bubbles of spit appeared at the corners of his mouth and Colette shivered. She couldn't bear the thought of going with him, and the stout woman was as bad. She didn't like the countess either, but as a sewing maid, she'd at least be free and earning a wage.

'Fetch your things, girl,' the countess snapped at Colette, and then she flinched sideways, her face suddenly contorted in disgust. The tortoiseshell cat was rubbing up against the countess's fur-lined mantle, purring so loudly that Colette could almost feel the vibrations in the air.

Colette smiled at the cat, but the countess hissed, and kicked out savagely with one pointed, jewelled shoe. The cat skittered back, not quite quickly enough, and mewed in pain. Then it began to drag itself away to the shadows under the bridge. The countess watched it, her face venomous under her pretty mask.

There was a moment of surprised silence. Cats were a nuisance, of course, stealing food and lying around in patches of sun just waiting to be stepped on, but most people in the city tolerated the strays that haunted the little alleyways. Gangs of boys might chase them for fun, but adults mostly sighed, and walked round them. Occasionally, people even left out scraps.

Colette stepped back, folding her hands neatly. The black tip of a patched, motley tail was trailing out from behind the stonework, and she fixed her eyes on it. 'I can't come with you, my lady,' she said, as politely as she could, while thinking of that kick. She had never been a huge lover of cats herself, and Ma had always said they were thieving brutes – Ma had threatened to turn that same tortoiseshell into a hat when she found it asleep on one of the showroom chairs. In the end she had chased it out with a broom, and told Colette that it was a cheeky devil, and too ugly even for skinning.

But the countess's face as she aimed that kick had been hateful – almost gloating. *An orphan child is probably not much more valuable than a stray cat*, Colette thought. 'My mother commended me to the care of the Guild. I must do as she wished.'

'Yes! Yes, indeed,' the old man muttered eagerly, and the stout woman surged forwards, drawing Colette against her apron and murmuring, 'Dear, good child!' She smelled of onions, but Colette pressed her face against the white linen, and did her best to look pious while sneaking a sideways look at the countess.

The countess stared back at her silently. She seemed almost confused, and Colette wondered if anyone ever said no to her. *What if she decides to kick the stout woman too?* Colette was going to laugh again. She fixed her eyes on the tail tip again, and tried to remember that she was an orphan.

'You are a very silly little girl,' the countess told Colette coldly, as she turned back towards her gondola. 'To turn down a position in my household, in favour of an *orphanage*.'

Colette nodded. 'I know it seems that way, my lady. But my mother...' She trailed off. She didn't want to keep repeating the lie. Ma had never said anything about the orphanage, and all she said about the Guild was that the dues were crippling. She had paid them because she had to, to be taken as a respectable dressmaker. Colette hoped that the countess would assume she was too upset to talk. Or perhaps she wouldn't even think about it – after all, Colette's feelings were too unimportant for her to worry about.

'An official from the Guild will wait on you, my lady.' The old man hurried to the edge of the canal.

'For the payment the child's mother was owed.' The countess simply stared straight ahead, as if she couldn't hear him, and he hurried along the bank as the gondola glided away, trying to keep up. 'The gold, my lady!' He stood balanced at the very edge of the paving stones, looking uncertain, as if he were considering jumping in after her, in case the gold should get away. Then he turned back, shoulders drooping, and nodded sharply at Colette. 'Pack your things, child.'

Colette bobbed a curtsey. 'Sir, my mother's workroom – all the materials. I must pack them up properly. Shall I bring them with me to the orphanage? Some of them could be sold, perhaps.'

The old man and the stout woman exchanged a glance, and Colette saw him rub his hands, one over the other. His eyes brightened and he nodded. 'Indeed. Indeed.'

'I could come to the orphanage tomorrow, with what I can carry,' Colette suggested. 'And a boat could come for the rest. There are some bales of fabric…'

'Most satisfactory,' the old man purred, and the stout woman pinched Colette's cheek. They hurried off down the *calle*, clearly quite pleased with their afternoon's work.

'All your poor ma's things,' Alyssa murmured sadly. 'Going to those old skinflints. I tell you this, Colette, I don't expect you orphans will see much of your ma's money. Not with those two in charge.'

Colette sighed. 'I know. Wait here a minute, Alyssa.' She hurried back inside, and returned a few moments later with a neat little silk hussif, folded around several gleaming needles. 'Here. Ma would have wanted you to have something.'

'But, Colette, don't you want her sewing things?' Alyssa stroked the silk pocket covetously, but she held it out to Colette again.

'She made me my own,' Colette explained. 'And – and I'd like to think of someone remembering her, Alyssa. Her and me.'

'Don't you worry, my dear. Whatever that dried-up old stick says, I shall come and visit you. I shan't need a needlecase to remind me of little Colette.'

Colette smiled sadly, and nodded, and let Alyssa hug her again. But she thought that Alyssa would need the hussif to remember her old neighbour, even though she couldn't tell her so. She didn't intend to be anywhere near this house, or the Guild orphanage, by the morning.

CHAPTER FOUR

COLETTE LOCKED THE OUTER DOOR of the shop, and hooked the heavy shutters closed with trembling fingers. Then she stood with her back against the wooden shutter, gazing into the rustling shadows of the showroom. If she half closed her eyes, she could see herself and Ma, flitting through the room over and over again, their arms full of cloth, mouths stuffed with pins, fussing and patting at their customers.

Colette pressed her hands over her eyes to shut the

shadows out, and gasped. She hadn't realised how hard it would be – that as well as losing Ma, she was losing the place where all her memories had been made.

She blundered across to the counter, where the ribbons were stored, to light a candle. She didn't have long. The Guild would be expecting her in the morning, so by then she must be hidden far away. She didn't know exactly where she was going – but she thought perhaps Burano, the lacemakers' island – she had enough small coins in Ma's purse to pay a boatman to take her. She had been there before with Ma, to buy lace for the shop. Ma had paid one of the old women to show them a few simple stitches, so they could make their own lace trimming. They would never be able to make the sort of lace that someone like the countess would want on her dresses and shifts, but the cheap ribbon lace sold well, and Colette loved making it. She could let her mind drift after a while, while her fingers twisted and knotted. Sometimes she had found that there were patterns in the lace that she hadn't planned, and she didn't know how she'd made them. But those pieces sold best of all.

Surely she could find work there, as an apprentice? Or even as a servant? She wouldn't mind, as long as she was far away from the Guild, and the countess – and yes, from the city and her memories too.

She began to move slowly around the showroom, stacking lengths of fabric on the counter, and gathering ribbons and the laces she had made into a bag. She supposed that the Guild orphanage would take the fabrics – they probably would be sold, as she had suggested, even if she weren't there herself. Or perhaps the landlord would seize them. They weren't very behind with the rent – no more than everyone else in the neighbourhood – but he was owed a month. Colette allowed herself a tiny smile at the thought of their landlord, who was rather good-looking and knew it, and who had tried for years to charm her mother, never really understanding that he wasn't getting anywhere. She could just imagine him and the dusty old man from the Guild orphanage squabbling on the steps of the Palazzo Morezzi. She didn't think either of them would get very far. The countess was bound to have armies of servants just to keep away unwelcome visitors. The Guild would probably have to go to law to get back the gold for the dress.

Colette left the showroom, knowing that she had really only been putting off what she needed to do. She paused at the door of the workroom, looking at their rickety old chairs, and the workboxes – hers and her mother's. She fetched out a large wicker basket, and began to pack. If she turned up in Burano with at least some tools of her trade, surely that would help? She began to tuck threads and skeins of silk into her basket. The heavy fabric shears. Her workbox and Ma's – she couldn't bear to leave that behind, even if she might never bring herself to use Ma's things. She opened up the little polished wooden box, and lifted out the velvet tray that fitted over the top. Ma's scissors and thimble were there, and everything she needed often. But underneath – Colette stirred the odd litter of objects, and sighed. There was a tiny little leather slipper in there, that she knew was one of her own, though she didn't remember wearing it.

She went on sifting through the box and then laughed in delighted surprise, pulling out a ragged, wooden doll, the paint on her face almost completely rubbed away. Colette hadn't seen her in years. She wore a faded dress of sprigged cotton – Colette had had one the same. Ma had done that, she remembered now, her eyes filling with tears. Whenever Colette had a new dress, she had made a tiny one for the doll too. That dress had been one of her favourites: creamy cotton, with tiny little green leaves scattered across it. Ma had made it with a full skirt, and Colette had loved to twirl in it.

Colette tucked the doll safely into her basket, and went on searching through the workbox. She picked out a small parcel wrapped in a faded bit of print fabric, thinking that it might be another slipper, or a bit of precious embroidery wrapped up to be kept safe. She unfolded the brittle cloth, and jumped back with a hiss, throwing the glittery handful away from her as if it were a spider, or a mouse.

So that was where it had gone. She had always wondered. The golden mask shimmered, even in the dusty corner where it had landed, under a stool.

She didn't want to pick it up – but it had been Ma's.

She was standing, looking at it, when she heard the noise. First, footsteps across the *calle*, and then a silence – a silence that Colette could feel, that she knew was someone hesitating outside the door of the shop. Whoever it was rattled the handle of the door gently to and fro – and then Colette heard the unmistakable click of the lock turning, the tumblers falling inside the door. The person outside had a key. Or they had unlocked the door some other way.

Colette stood frozen, unsure whether to shout out and challenge them, or to run upstairs and hide.

It must be a thief – someone who had heard that the strange English dressmaker had died, and her child had been taken off to the orphanage. They were hoping for easy pickings from an empty house. *You're too early*, Colette thought angrily. *The rumours went ahead of themselves. I'm still here.* She wasn't going to run, she realised, clenching her fists. She couldn't just leave them to steal Ma's things. But neither was she brave enough to confront the thief.

Shaking, Colette crept towards the door to the showroom, wondering if she could work some spell to scare away the thief. All she knew were sewing spells, but her golden fish had moved like real ones, and she had seen magic in the blue silk dress, and that girl's mask. There was a chance that she could do something useful, surely.

She peered cautiously around the door, and her heart raced to a sickening speed as she saw a dark form stooping over the counter, picking at her bag of laces. Colette bit her lower lip between her teeth to stop herself from shouting at the figure. She hated to see someone riffling through her precious things!

Then the dark figure straightened up and turned, looking straight at her. Colette froze. The burglar couldn't see her, surely? It was just chance that he was looking that way. Unless he'd heard her – had she made the door creak?

'Come out.' The voice was low, and surprisingly pleasant. The thief didn't sound at all as Colette had expected a thief would. She kept still, though. Perhaps he was only bluffing, and he couldn't see her at all.

'Yes, you. Behind the door. Come here.'

Colette felt her feet twitch, and there was a strange, pleasant sleepiness in her head – something that told her she should do as he said, that it was quite all right.

'No!' She stamped her feet, one after the other, stamping away the twitches, and shook her head so her hair slapped around her face. 'No, I won't!'

But she *was* moving – in tiny steps towards the man. She was almost sure she could see him smiling. *Smirking*.

'You should be ashamed, robbing an orphan,' she

snarled. 'My mother only died three days ago, haven't you any decency?'

'If I were a thief, Colette, I would say no, I hadn't – decency not being a useful characteristic for thieves. Luckily for you, I'm not.'

'Oh. You're not?' Colette gathered her wits, and put her hands on her hips to glare at him better. At least he seemed to have stopped dragging her towards him now. 'What are you doing creeping around my ma's shop in the dark, then?' She paused for a moment, and blinked. 'And how do you know my name?'

'Bring the candle here, Colette,' the man said calmly. 'You'll see.'

Colette felt like stamping her foot again, but in the end she only hissed in frustration, and whirled around to fetch the candle. She held it up between them, and snapped, 'What?'

'Look at me.' He pulled back the hood of his black cloak, and Colette stared at him, wondering what on earth she was supposed to see. He looked a perfectly normal sort of man – he didn't look particularly criminal, she supposed. Was that what he was trying to show her?

Then her breath caught in her chest, and she remembered those hours she'd spent, staring into the water, staring at herself. The man's hair was brushed back, and tied in a tail at the nape of his neck, where it curled a little. He hadn't powdered it, like a fashionable noble, and it shone red-gold in the candlelight. He had hazel eyes that glittered as Colette gazed into them.

'Do you know who I am?' he asked her gently.

'Ma said that you were dead,' Colette murmured. 'If you're who I think you must be…'

'Since she refused to see me, after we parted, I might as well have been,' the man said bitterly. 'She and I did not agree, Colette. On many things, we discovered. But I *am* your father.'

Colette stared back at him, her heart thumping. She had imagined so many things – but she had never thought that her father might still be alive. Ma had told her so many times that he had died. Yet, here he was – she could see the resemblance. Bewildered, she gazed into the glitter of his eyes, and felt herself smile.

Then she wiped the smile away, and scowled instead. That had been a charm – he had been making her like him, charming her like a bird out of a tree. What if this was all just a lie? Some elaborate plot?

Colette thought furiously. Why, though? Who would hatch such a silly scheme, just to steal an orphan? And besides, she really could see the likeness. But that didn't mean she had to fall into his hands, like a helpless little bird.

'What sort of things did you not agree on?' she asked suspiciously, raising the candle higher to look more closely into his face.

'Magic.'

'You're a magician?' Colette burst out eagerly, all at once forgetting to be cautious. 'Is that – could that be – I met one of the water horses, and she said…' She stopped, looking at him hopefully.

'You have magic in you too,' he told her. 'I can see

it. What did Harriet – your mother, I mean – what did she say about me?'

'Nothing,' said Colette, with a sigh. 'Just that you were dead. I never knew that you were a magician. I thought the strange things I saw were just…strange.'

The man made an odd noise, as if he felt like spitting. 'For a time, Colette, I loved your mother dearly. But she had the most foolish ideas about magic. She should not have tried to keep it away from you. What did she think would happen?' he muttered, almost to himself. He came closer, and leaned down to look Colette in the eyes. 'I'm sorry. She was so angry with me, and we fought so badly when you were a tiny child. I left… I shouldn't have. But I had it in my head that you were too young to know, anyway. I always meant to come back and talk to Harriet, to explain to her that I had to see you, before your magic began to show. I left it too late.' He looked at the black bands stitched around Colette's sleeves, and grimaced. 'Much too late.'

Colette nodded. It was only just beginning to settle

into her mind that she had a father. And that her mother had indeed been lying all those years.

And that, perhaps, she didn't need to run away after all. 'Why – why are you here?' she asked huskily. 'Did you hear about my mother?'

'Yes. If I'd known earlier, I would have come to the funeral, of course. But the news only reached me tonight.' He lowered his head – almost bowing to her. 'Colette, you don't know me. But I am your father – you can see that I am. Even though your mother and I fought, she would have wanted me to look after you.'

'I'm supposed to go to the orphanage run by the Tailors' Guild,' Colette murmured. 'But I was going to run away. Tonight. Although Countess Morezzi did offer me a place in her household as a sewing maid,' she added, standing a little straighter. She wanted him to know that she was old enough to have her own place in the world. He wasn't taking on a little girl.

'Countess Morezzi?' His eyes glittered in the

candlelight, and Colette took a tiny step back.

'Yes...'

'You said no?'

'She kicked a cat... I know that sounds stupid, but her face was – frightening.'

'I can well imagine,' he murmured. 'I can't tell whether that was clever of you or not, Colette. I have done work for her in the past...she's a strange woman. Very powerful in court circles, but she has no magic whatsoever. She tries to borrow other people's instead.'

'What sort of work do you do?' Colette asked curiously. 'Are you a...a magician for hire?' She frowned. That didn't sound quite right.

'I'm a maskmaker. But the masks I create are special.' Colette saw him flinch, and then he smiled. 'Colette, that's your mother's face. I thought you looked like me, but just then it could have been her disapproving look.'

'I've never worn a mask,' Colette said carefully, trying not to let her dislike of the things show so clearly again. 'I'm a little bit frightened of them, I think.'

He smiled at her. 'There *is* something unnerving about them – no eyes, I suppose. But, remember, Colette, it's the person behind the mask that you should think of, not the mask itself.' It sounded as though he'd said this many times, but Colette wrinkled her nose.

'That's all very well, but the masks don't help. Don't you think that people behave worse when they have masks on?' She shivered. 'Because no one knows who they are, and they think they can get away with anything.' She bit her bottom lip, looking up at him. 'I shouldn't have said that… Are you sure you want me to be your daughter?'

'Indeed I do, Colette. You remind me of your mother, very much.'

'My mother that you fought with all the time.'

'Your mother that I fought with all the time, but loved dearly, even when we were throwing things at each other,' he agreed.

Colette gasped, with laughter and dismay. 'You *threw* things?'

'I threw things by magic, which were carefully spelled not to hurt,' he pointed out. 'Your mother just threw things and assumed that I would duck.'

It was so odd to hear him talk of her mother like this. Colette wasn't sure she could even imagine it. Her mother had always been such a solitary person. She had friends among the neighbours, but no one close. Certainly no one she cared deeply enough about to throw things at. 'She ripped my sewing up, sometimes,' she said suddenly. 'If she thought I wasn't trying. But not for years. And I'm a better embroiderer than her – I mean, I was. I think that was the magic. My embroidery started to move, you see.'

'Will you come with me?' her father asked, and Colette studied him. She knew from watching other children, and hearing them talk, that this was not how fathers spoke. They ordered, they did not ask. But she supposed her father was in a strange position now. Was he even her father, legally, as she had never lived with him? He could probably disown her, if he decided that he didn't want her.

'What will I do?' she asked suddenly.

He looked around the workroom – at the rickety chairs, and the yellowed whitewash on the walls. 'My masks, luckily, are in great demand.' Colette frowned at him. He seemed to be picking his way towards something, very carefully. 'Your mother, being English, and a woman on her own, was never appreciated in this city the way she should have been—'

'You're trying to say that you're richer than her,' Colette put in. 'You really didn't need to tell me that. Your cloak is made of velvet, and there's a diamond in the lace at your throat. I don't want to be a little child who has' – she paused, trying to think of what her spoiled little clients did – 'dancing lessons.'

'Don't you like to dance?' he asked lightly. 'Oh, I know what you mean. Again, you remind me of your mother. I tried to persuade her that she did not need to work. That was one of our greatest arguments.'

'She loved to sew. If you tried to stop her…'

He shrugged. 'It was stupid. It was a matter of pride. I wanted to provide for her.'

'I want to work,' Colette told him stubbornly, and he nodded.

'Yes. You shall, I promise. What do you need to bring with you?'

Colette slung the bag of ribbons on top of the basket where she had placed the two workboxes. She was wearing her only dress that properly fitted, but she had folded up a spare shift, and some stockings. It was all she had. Except for the remnants of blue silk. She brought them out, laying them gently in the basket, and her father whistled, a low, hissed breath of surprise.

'We made a dress out of it, for the Countess Morezzi. She never paid,' Colette told him. 'I knew she wouldn't, the silk told me. I saw pictures…' She shuddered, remembering those images of Ma. But the silk hadn't got it quite right – Ma had died before the countess could cheat her.

'It's beautiful,' he murmured. 'I heard about that dress – embroidered all over with golden fish, so beautifully sewn that when she twirled her skirts in the dance, the fish seemed to dance too. There was a lot of talk about it, after the countess's party.' He smiled at her, proudly. 'That was you?'

'That was me,' Colette agreed quietly. She couldn't help smiling. People had been talking about her work.

'Is this all?' He looked at the meagre basket in surprise.

'I could take the fabrics.' Colette looked around the showroom. 'But these are the only things I really want to bring. Are we going now?' Her voice went thin as she said it. She had been planning to leave, but now the house seemed small and warm and safe, and so full of pictures of herself and Ma. 'Oh…' She had caught sight of the golden mask, sparkling at her from its corner. 'Did you make this?' she murmured, picking up the scrap of fabric, and using it to scoop the mask into her hands. She held it out, and her father sighed.

'She kept it, then,' he whispered. 'I did wonder – I made it for her as a courting gift.' He smiled, reaching for it, and stroked the shining threads. 'May I, Colette?'

She pressed it into his hands, glad to be relieved of the responsibility – she hadn't wanted to take it, or to leave it behind. The thing could go back to its maker.

'Yes.' He picked up the basket, and tucked it under his arm. Then he held out his other hand to her.

Colette looked around, and then took a deep breath and blew out the candle. She put her hand in her father's, and followed him through the darkened shop, out to the *calle*. He led her towards the bridge, and Colette looked back at the shop, with its neat gilt lettering across the door.

A faint rustling made her look down at the balustrade of the bridge, and she smiled to see the tortoiseshell cat. It didn't look hurt – it was sitting neatly and smugly on the stonework, with its thin tail wrapped around its paws.

She held out one hand, just to gently touch it under the chin, and it nodded to her gravely. As she followed her father over the bridge, she could see the cat still watching her, yellow eyes gleaming.

Chapter Five

Her first glimpse of the shop was by lamp-light. They had burst suddenly out of a dark, narrow alley, down from the jetty on the Grand Canal where the hired boatman had left them. The little square in front of the grand church of San Moise had been brightly lit, making Colette blink owlishly and stare around. The whole front of the church was covered in carvings, of people and strange beasts, and they seemed to shimmer and move in the dancing light, just like her fish.

'Do you like it?' Her father looked at her, smiling. 'A lot of people say it's ugly – and that it was only built to glorify the family that paid for it. But it makes me smile.'

'What are those things?' Colette asked, twisting her head sideways to look at the long-necked beasts above the door.

'Camels. But I have seen a camel, in a travelling menagerie, and it did not look like that.' Her father shook his head and laughed. 'But then, I couldn't draw one.'

Colette frowned at the camels. She wasn't sure she could sew one, either – not if they really looked like that. She looked around the little piazza, admiring the freshly swept stones, and the pretty lamp-brackets. Even the light itself was golden and clear, not like the smoking torches that lit her old neighbourhood. 'Are those lamps *magic*?' she asked, staring at the lights in surprise.

Her father nodded. 'Yes. We local shopkeepers pay for their upkeep. It's good for business – people feel safe here, and it means the shops can open after dark. Here, look. This is my shop.'

Colette peered at it, reading the bright sign that ran above the door. *Mascheria Sorani.* Then she saw the masks, staring out at her, their empty eyes catching her own. Her hand tightened in her father's, but he was smiling down at her so proudly, so keen to show her his work that she couldn't say anything. She could only smile and nod.

The masks seemed to watch her as they approached the door. The shop was double fronted, with two silk-draped windows. The masks were laid against the silk, like ornaments. Most of them were so finely carved and jewelled that they would have fitted in any drawing room.

How could they be looking at her, when they had no eyes? Colette followed her father into the shop, a velvet-lined jewel box of a place. Clearly only the richest of clients came to the Mascheria Sorani. There were more of the magic lanterns on the walls, and their light shimmered over overstuffed velvet chairs, and walls hung with gilded papers.

Her father waved a hand at it dismissively. 'This is just for the clients. The real heart of the place is the workshop, on the first floor. Then there are bedrooms up above.' He smiled at her. 'You'll think me foolish, but there is a room for you. I furnished it a long time ago – but you may think it looks like a room for one of those little girls who have dancing lessons.'

Colette smiled at him. She was delighted – he hadn't forgotten her! He had wanted her all along… But at the same time, the slightly suspicious, common-sense voice was whispering inside her. It was a voice that made her feel as if her mother was still there.

If her father had wanted her so much, why had he not made more of an effort to find her?

Colette slept late the next morning, exhausted by the flurry of packing and then the late-night trip across the city with the stranger who was her father.

She had been woken at last by a faint scratching at the door, and she sat up, gazing around at the strangeness of her pretty, rich girl's room.

The door was opening, and a girl peered around the edge of it, smiling at her. Colette hadn't met any of the other members of the household the night before – everyone had been asleep. Her father had half carried her up the stairs to her room, and Colette had crawled into the embroidered bed by the faint light of a candle.

'You're awake then,' the girl murmured, walking in and holding out a tray. A painted tray with a cup of chocolate, and biscuits, just like a grand lady. Just as she had imagined the countess. Colette tried to smile at the maid, but she thought she might only be making a strange sort of grimace.

It was all too strange.

'When you want to get up, Mistress Colette—' *Mistress?* Colette gaped at her. 'The master sent Lina out for some clothes for you. He says you'll have better ones made, but these will do for now.' She darted out, returning with an armful of pale, delicate fabrics – fine linen and silk – which she laid gently in the huge wooden press at the foot of the bed. 'Will you need my help to dress?' she asked Colette, who was still staring at her. 'My name is Maria, mistress.'

'Colette. I m-mean, please call me Colette,' Colette stammered, and Maria frowned.

'I'm not sure, mistress,' she murmured. 'A moment, while I fetch your washing water.'

Colette watched her dark skirts whisk around the door, and leaned back against her feather pillows, anxiously picking at the embroidered cover of her bed. She had never expected anything like this. Servants, and silk dresses. Was this what her mother had fought against? It seemed ungrateful, to complain that everything was too nice. Colette sipped her chocolate, and made a face. Too sweet.

She put the thin china bowl on the table beside the bed, and slid out from under the covers. *I'm like Ma*, she thought to herself, with a sideways smile. *How is it that I'd rather dip stale bread in yesterday's warmed-*

up coffee than nibble on sweet biscuits and chocolate?

'You're up!' Maria set down a steaming jug of water.

'Yes.' Colette nodded determinedly. 'Thank you for the water.'

'And you're sure, about dressing yourself?' Maria smiled at the expression on Colette's face. 'Yes, then…' She nodded to Colette, and backed away to the door with the merest hint of a curtsey, just a quick bend of the knees.

Colette wrapped her arms tightly around her chest, and blinked sleep-heavy eyes. Maria had curtseyed to her. Almost, anyway. She shook her head in disbelief, and splashed her face with the warm water, hoping it would clear her thoughts.

Dressed in the plainest of her new dresses – she was tempted to wear her own old things, but it would seem like a calculated insult to her father – Colette padded uncertainly downstairs. She didn't even know where to go.

Her father appeared, smiling, as she reached the

last step, and stroked a hand admiringly down her cheek, almost as if he were petting a dog. Colette smiled back a little uncertainly. The room, and the clothes – they were beautiful. But she didn't know what she was supposed to do in return.

'Sir!' A boy appeared, leaning over the stairs. 'Sir, you'd better come, that spell's unravelling, and I don't—'

Colette's father cursed sharply and galloped past her up the stairs towards the boy. *So their workroom is up there, then*, Colette thought, staring after him. *Should I follow?* No one had said… She nibbled a wisp of her hair, and then stepped down into the passage instead, peeking around the door of the shop, and then down the passage that led to the kitchen quarters. But she didn't feel she belonged there, either.

Uncertainly, she crept back up the stairs, and sat hidden around the turn of the staircase, watching Maria and the other maid, Lina, darting back and forth, and hearing the gossip and busyness in and out of the shop. A little carillon of golden bells rang every time the shop door opened, and one of the shop clerks would swoop on the customers, bowing and murmuring, ready to show them mask after mask, each one more beautiful and expensive than the last.

The shop had been busy, but there had been no customers who were important enough for the maskmaker himself to see them. Colette could see the door of the workroom too, on the first floor, but it stayed closed all morning – presumably they were still dealing with the unravelling spell? Colette longed to see what it was, but she didn't dare knock on the door. Not yet.

She ate a quick midday meal with her father and his apprentice, Rizzo. He was a tall, haughty-looking boy with dark curly hair. So far he'd not said anything to Colette beyond 'Good day', but he kept looking at her sideways. Rather sadly, Colette had realised that he wasn't going to like her much, either. Why would he want his master's spoiled little daughter hanging about? Until she arrived, he would have been the maskmaker's favourite, and now he had been replaced.

She listened to them talking about the troublesome spell, wishing that she understood the strange, lyrical terms they dropped in like jewels. Then she listened to the same conversation at dinner time, after she had slipped out through the shop to explore the streets around her new home. She sat there, nibbling the grandest food she had ever eaten, and listened, and didn't say anything. Except, *Oh, yes, indeed*, when her father asked if she had everything as she liked it in her room. How could she say anything else? It was more than she had said to anyone all day.

The shop itself was not that much larger than Colette and her ma's, but the street it was on was fashionable, and busy, not like their little backwater. It was taller too. There were rooms piled on rooms up a narrow, twisting staircase. Rooms for sleeping, and rooms full of stores and fabrics and strange substances that Colette wasn't sure about at all. They came in bales and boxes and jars, with labels in a variety of crabbed and spidery writings, and many of them smelled quite odd.

Her own room was beautiful. So beautiful that it didn't feel to Colette as though it could possibly belong to her. It really *was* a room for one of those little girls whose dresses she had embroidered. She and Ma had made quite a lot of young girls' dresses, when families had not wanted to use the expensive tailors just for the children. Colette could imagine that those girls had rooms like this, and that they left them scattered with dolls, and squashed hats, and books with torn pages, but she was planning to keep hers pristine. When her father had opened the door that first night to show it to her, a gust of rather stale, scented air had rushed out at her. No one had slept in this room, he explained. It had been kept just for Colette. Still, she'd woken up this second morning and found it hard to believe that the room was hers – that she wasn't supposed to be doing mending for the child who really slept here.

Colette sat bunched up in the four-poster bed,

with its stiff silk curtains, and peered around the room, admiring it all over again. The bed's curtains were a creamy pink silk, embroidered with neat little bunches of darker pink and green flowers. She hadn't drawn them shut the night before – it was too odd, sleeping in a scented, silken cave. It made it too hard to breathe. It made her think of Ma. It was still quite early, but Colette didn't want to laze in bed, even though she could. It was too strange, going from life as a hardworking seamstress, to the petted only child of a well-known magician. A well-known and exceedingly well-to-do magician, so it seemed. When her father had told her that he was a maskmaker, Colette had assumed that he was a craftsman, much like the tailors and hatters whose shops she passed every day. Someone who sold their work, much as Ma had. But Giacomo Sorani was more than that. He was the city's foremost magical maskmaker – and the ladies and gentlemen of the Venetian court were desperate for Sorani masks.

Her father employed an apprentice, two shop

clerks, a messenger boy and a cook, as well as the two serving maids, Maria and Lina. Colette was fairly sure that Maria, who would be bringing up her washing water in a few minutes, was only a couple of years older than she was. Maria was perfectly polite, but this had to be strange for her too, Colette thought. *Why should she have to wait on me? She knows I'm not used to it. I expect she sniggers about me to Lina in the kitchen.*

Without realising what she was doing, Colette traced her fingers over the embroidery on the counterpane of her bed. It was decorated with the same little bunches of flowers as the bed curtains. They weren't as Colette would have made them. They were a pattern, that was all – a repeating design of the same shapes and colours that said nothing about the way the flowers really looked. It made Colette cross – so much work had gone into them, hours and hours of stitching, days of strained eyes and bleeding fingers and that hateful, hunched pain across the back of the seamstress's shoulders. Colette could practically see her, shut up in a workshop somewhere here in the city, squinting in the candlelight at the fussy little pattern. Why hadn't she just *looked*? She sighed. The girl would have been tired, and hungry, and afraid of her mistress. She had followed the pattern she'd been given obediently, and no magic had risen up in her fingers to bring those flowers to life. *But she'd have been as frightened as I was, if it had*, Colette thought. *I was lucky, though. I wouldn't give the magic back.* It was the first time that she had been grateful. *I am lucky, truly I am. Even though it doesn't feel that way, without Ma. At least I'm not alone.*

She nodded to herself, and the silk threads loosed themselves as she scrunched her hands into the fabric, and began to wind around her fingertips. Colette pulled her hands away with a gasp, and watched as the strands of silk coiled helplessly in the air, suddenly deprived of the magic that had uprooted them from their pattern. They seemed to sniff the air, and then they collapsed again, lying limp and tangled on the satin bedspread.

Colette stared down at them in dismay. However much she disliked the formal, unimaginative design, it had probably been very expensive – and now it was ruined, and in a few minutes the maid was going to arrive with her washing water, and see.

'Go back!' Colette hissed to the threads, but nothing happened. They stayed trailing across the satin, looking bedraggled. Reluctantly, Colette pressed her fingers back against the bedspread – and, at once, she felt the strands of silk begin to coil and twist, tickling her fingertips. 'Go back. You know how to, just the way you were before. Those silly little bunches. Oh, go on!' Colette slapped her hand crossly against that satin. 'There's no time. Please?' She gasped in a little breath of relief as the threads began to move again, purposefully this time. She closed her eyes, and smiled at the faint glow of summer sunlight on her eyelids. *Flowers*. She would think of flowers – surely that would help speed the magic along? There were gardens in Venice – they weren't places for seamstresses' daughters, they were for the nobility, and they had high walls, and guards – but plants climbed walls, and burrowed through cracks, and clambered through railings. She had seen them, spilling swathes of bright, acid colour out into the street. Ma had loved those gaudy peacock plants. She had lifted Colette so she could sniff them, and taught her to love them too. Whenever she was out on her errands, Colette had touched the flowers, cupped the petals in her hands, stroked them and counted them, and thought about how she would weave them into her work. Not in a tidy repeating pattern, but sprawling gorgeously across silk that was the colour of the faded stucco of a palazzo wall. *A creamy pink…*

'Mistress Colette!'

Colette opened her eyes and stared guiltily at Maria, wondering what she had done. 'Oh… I meant to get up, before you came. I'm sorry.'

'You don't need to be sorry, miss. It's my job to wake you,' the maid said tartly. 'The master never said that you could do it too…'

Colette blinked at her, and looked down at her

hands, to where Maria was staring. They were spread out across the counterpane, small hands, with sewing calluses and neat, short nails. But her skinny fingers were hardly visible, hidden under the layers of fine embroidery thread that had grown over them like ivy.

'Oh…' she whispered. That wasn't what she had meant at all…

'Can you even get out of that?' Maria asked, setting down the steaming jug of hot water on Colette's wash stand, and coming closer to peer at the bedspread.

'I don't know,' Colette admitted. The neat pattern of posies had completely disappeared from both bedspread and curtains now. Instead, a luxuriant mass of creepers sprawled across them, studded with tiny, bright flowers.

'Is that jasmine?' Maria asked, tracing one stem. 'I don't know all these. That's what your magic is then, miss?'

'It's only just starting to show,' Colette whispered. 'My ma didn't like it. The magic, that is. She'd have liked the flowers… I didn't mean to do this, honestly,

I didn't. The pattern was so – so boring, and then it started to change, and I tried to put it back…'

'Looks like it,' Maria muttered. 'You'll fit in properly here, anyway. Between the master and that Rizzo and now you, we'd better watch out.' She sighed. 'Do you need me to unpick you, miss? Shall I fetch some scissors?'

Colette smiled hopefully at Maria, and twisted her hands gently against the embroidered stems. 'I might. I'll try to get out of it myself first, but if that doesn't work…'

Maria crouched down by the bed, staring at Colette's fingers. 'You could mend stockings like that,' she murmured. 'Imagine, just having to think your darning done.'

'I suppose I could,' Colette agreed. 'Except I might end up with my stockings all covered in flowers. Or who knows what else.' She glared at the embroidery twisting in and out of her fingers, and a few of the tightest threads wisped out of the silk, wafting and twirling as if they were tasting the magic in the air.

They restitched themselves into a neat little flower, and Colette eased her hands away, rubbing them thoughtfully.

'Do my father and his apprentice do things like that all the time?' she asked Maria. 'Is that why you said I'd fit in?'

The older girl shrugged. 'We mostly stay out of the workshop. Rizzo sweeps it – or he magics the dust away, I don't know. But all sorts goes on in there. Not all of it as harmless as changing around the embroideries on a set of bed hangings, either. And don't you go telling your father I said so,' she added in a snap.

'I won't,' Colette promised her humbly. 'Maria,' she called, as the maid went to the door. 'I can try and mend your stockings, if you like. I don't know how they'd turn out, but I'd do my best.'

Maria laughed. 'I'll see.'

Colette watched her go, and sighed. She could have been friends with Maria and Lina if she had gone to the countess's house as a sewing maid, or the Guild orphanage had apprenticed her out. She might have met one of the maids out in the market, or the countess could have sent her to pick up a mask. They could have gossiped about the countess and the maskmaker, and the strange, irritating habits of their households, the things that servants had to put up with.

It wasn't that Colette particularly wanted to be a maid, or even an apprentice. The countess would have been the most terrifying mistress, and the Guild would probably have sent her as an apprentice to someone who thought they could get more work out of an orphan. Of course she was better off where she was. It was just…it would be pleasant to have someone to talk to. Even when she and Ma had argued, which had been often, they had never gone for long without sharing a quick roll of the eyes over a customer wanting yet more knots of ribbon, or another layer of flounces, or a dress the colour of the one their neighbour had, but better. She couldn't – for the moment – imagine doing that with her father. It was hard even to think of him as her father. Colette found herself calling him 'the maskmaker' even in her head. He had swooped down and rescued her, and then tucked her away in this pretty room.

Colette had no sense of what she was supposed to do now, except that it would be better not to redecorate the rest of the house as well.

I'm lonely, she thought to herself with surprise, as she pulled back the flower-strewn coverlet. *Even though there are more people here than I've ever shared a house with before.*

As Colette did up the laces of her bodice, she decided that today she would have to find something to do. She couldn't just keep on sitting on the stairs and watching. Her father had promised that she would be able to work, but he hadn't mentioned anything about it. Perhaps he thought that now he had brought her here, she would sit in that pretty room like a songbird in a cage, and he could admire her. She was there to make him smile. Colette sniffed, and tucked her hair tightly under her cap. More likely, now he knew that she was safe, he'd just forgotten she was there, like he'd forgotten about her for the last ten years. A small smile curved her lips, and she marched to the door, yanking it open with a determined heave. She hurried down the staircase almost too fast for safety, tripping over her feet and catching at the wall. Today she would *not* sit quietly and watch from the steps. They would have to give her something to do. Even if it were only tidying up the workroom. To start with.

She stood hesitating on the landing, telling herself that she was only catching her breath. She had felt so determined, up in her room, but now the closed door looked daunting, and the room beyond it seemed completely silent. If she knocked, she suspected her father or the apprentice would simply shout at her to go away, that they were not to be disturbed; or perhaps there would be no answer at all, which would be worse. So it was better not to knock – just to unlatch the door and slip inside before anyone could stop her.

Colette sucked her stomach in, trying to take up as

little space as possible as she slid around the door. She was going to make them listen to her – of course she was. But she wanted a good look at the workroom first. She stood in the shadows by the door, peering into the dimness of the room. They had shutters across all the windows, she realised, so that only thin lines of light filtered through into the room. Her father and his apprentice were stooped over a long central table, their work lit by branches of fine wax candles.

Colette held back a disapproving sniff. Why shut out the sunlight, and burn candles so wastefully? Those were the best pale wax too, their flames a soft, steady glow and giving off a faint scent of honey, not the stink of tallow. The candlelight danced on the masks hanging all around the walls, so that their painted smiles lurched and Colette could swear they turned to look at her.

Perhaps she didn't hold back the sniff quite enough. Her father glanced round, his face eerily lit by the candles, so that his eyes glittered out of shadowy pits. 'Child! What are you doing here?'

Colette bobbed a curtsey to him, and smiled, like a sweet little daughter would. 'You said that there would be work for me to do, sir.'

'Yes… yes… but surely a few days of holiday first,' he murmured, looking back at his work as if he couldn't bear to leave it for more than a moment. 'Some time to mourn your mother…'

'I am mourning all the time,' Colette said, standing a little straighter. 'I don't see that I will ever stop thinking about her. So I had better mourn and work. I have never had a holiday, except perhaps a saint's day here and there. What would you like me to do?'

'Well…' The maskmaker gazed down at his creations, spread out over the bench.

Colette tried not to shudder as she stepped closer, looking over his shoulder at all those half-made faces.

'I could tidy up,' she suggested. Even in the candlelight, she could see that a thin film of plaster dust coated the table, and that the floor was littered with strips of paper, paintbrushes, feathers and scraps of fabric. Maria had said that it was Rizzo's job to clean the workroom, but Colette suspected that they simply never bothered.

'No, no…' her father murmured. 'Everything is in its place.'

Colette looked pointedly at the floor, but he didn't seem to notice. She could feel the apprentice, Rizzo, staring at her, and as her father looked vaguely around the room, she lifted her head to stare back. The boy glared at her, his eyes gleaming like marbles in the flickering light. Colette dragged her eyes away, casting them down demurely as her father turned to look at her again.

'Embroidery…' he murmured, stretching out a finger, and twirling it in one of the reddish coils of hair that sprang out from under Colette's cap. Colette stood still, but she felt a shiver run over her skin at his touch. Only Ma played with her hair. No one else. Her father's fingers were different – thinner and longer, with no calluses to catch on her hair. That odd, affectionate little gesture had opened up the giant hole in her chest again, where her mother had been torn away.

'Yes… We must train you, of course. There's nothing so dangerous as magic left unattended. But there isn't much sewing in the making of masks, Colette. Almost all the work is done with paint, and glue. The feathers and jewels are stuck to the leather or porcelain, you see.'

'What about veils?' Colette asked stubbornly, pushing down the ache inside her. She couldn't cry now – she had to make him listen. She had seen women wearing half-masks with black veils hanging underneath them. Surely they had to be sewn?

'Oh, we don't make those.' Her father waved a hand dismissively. 'A maid's job. No skill.'

Colette set her teeth together in a tight grimace to stop herself snarling. She could see a smirk around the mouth of that apprentice too, stupid beast.

'But what we do need' – her father was beaming at her now – 'what we *do* need, are ribbons. To tie on the masks. And I see no reason why we shouldn't have embroidered ones.' He looked at Colette with his head on one side, and seemed to see at last that she was disappointed. 'It will be very good practice for your growing magic, Colette. Do you think that ribbons are beneath you?'

'No... It's just – there's no space,' Colette explained. 'Ribbons are thin.'

'Exactly. So your spells will need to be neat and tidy. Perfectly fitted to the confines of a ribbon.' Her father nodded, pleased with himself. He looked as though he had been carefully planning this all along, instead of coming up with it as a desperate idea to keep an unexpected daughter busy. 'When your magic first begins to show, the most important lesson you must learn is control.' He swung around suddenly, and glared at his apprentice who was smirking openly at Colette now, enjoying the scene. 'Isn't it, Rizzo?' He turned back to smile at Colette. 'Two fires. And half the ceiling collapsed. Just in his first month. Don't let him tell you otherwise.'

Colette nodded, but remembering the bed cover

upstairs, she didn't let herself smirk back at Rizzo, however much she was tempted. 'Shall I fetch my workbox?' she murmured.

'Yes! Yes, at once. I don't know why I never thought of this before! Surely the ribbons should match the spells we paint onto the masks. Hurry, Colette!'

Colette scurried back up the stairs to fetch her embroidery threads. When she returned, she found that Rizzo had pulled a battered little sewing table out of some corner of the workroom, and set it up close to her father's stool. He was lighting another branch of candles, while the maskmaker himself burrowed in and out of the drawers set in a great wall chest. 'Here! Gauzes. Silk. Satin. All colours.' He heaped them in a glorious mess on Colette's table. 'Now, come here, and look at this mask, child. So you can choose a ribbon to fit, and work the spells into your stitching.'

Colette leaned over, resting her elbows on the high table to peer at their work. It was an ornate mask, half painted already. It glowed in the candlelight, a golden sun covering most of the face, but with a silvery moon circling it at the side. Golden rays waved out around half the face, and a spray of glittering stars trembled on the other. It wasn't only the candlelight that made it glow, Colette realised admiringly. It shone with a soft sun and moon light of its own. She turned her head to one side, and nodded. Each side of the mask gave out its own light. Then she gasped, and laughed, looking up at her father.

'You saw?' he asked, smiling.

'A shooting star!'

'Just every so often,' he agreed. 'A little extra touch. It's spelled into the moon paint, to skim over the face.'

'It's beautiful,' Colette murmured. She could see the spell, she realised now. There was a shifting in the silver paint of the moon face, an extra shimmer. When she reached out her hand to touch it, a tiny star danced in and out of her fingertips, and frosted her nails with silver.

'Those are the pretty details that our customers expect,' her father explained. 'Delicacy. Beauty. A little touch of mysterious magic here and there. Can you build a spell like that with silks, Colette? You'll need to coat every strand with a spell.' He took her hand, rubbing his thumb across her glittering nails, and began to whisper, his breath a warm gust against her palm. More stars appeared as he spoke, tiny points of light that danced around her hand. Colette felt something rise inside her, a desperate longing that she suddenly realised was her own untried magic, surging out of her to join with her father's practised skill. The stars swirled up around her head and seemed to sing in her ears and she laughed again, forgetting that dark emptiness of grief inside her for a moment. She could feel the spell on her lips and in her fingers, and she wanted to speak it aloud, so much – but her father pressed one long finger over her mouth.

'Not yet. Not yet. If you say it now, Colette, half my workshop will be blazing silver. Sit. Gather your tools. Then whisper it...'

Colette sighed delightedly as the silver stars faded into her skin, and then snatched at the pile of ribbons, her eyes searching hungrily for her needlecase. There was an itching in her fingers, and she drummed them restlessly against the table. 'Do you have any gold thread?' she murmured, eyeing a midnight-blue gauze that had trailed down onto the floor. She could hear their low whispers behind her as she settled into the chair Rizzo had set out by her sewing table and unwound the hank of golden thread that he had slapped down next to her. She could see the stars already, their pattern dancing across the gauze ribbon in a glittering constellation.

Colette wove the wisps of ribbon in and out of her fingers, smiling to herself at their silken delicacy. She almost forgot her loneliness as she began to stitch scattered stars across the ribbon – but not quite. The stars were lonely too, so diamond-cold and far away. Someone who had asked to hide behind a starry sky would know that, Colette was sure.

Chapter Six

'HAVEN'T YOU FINISHED THAT RIBBON yet? You've been working on it for days.' Rizzo stood looking down at the sewing table, his wide mouth twisted in a sneer.

Colette looked up at him, her fingers tightening on the coil of dark gauze ribbon. She didn't want to talk. She could be rude – there were plenty of sharp answers she could have snapped back – but she was tired, and she couldn't be bothered to fight. 'No,' she said flatly, and she stroked a tiny golden star. Her father had shown her a spell that would make it glitter, and she pressed into the bump of the stitching with her forefinger. She closed her eyes, feeling the pattern of the stitches dig into her skin and thinking the spell inside her head.

'What are you closing your eyes for?' Rizzo jeered. 'Can't you do the spell without? You really haven't inherited much from your father, have you?' He clicked his fingers together under her nose, and Colette saw the magic spring from his fingertips. The whole ribbon lit up in a mass of twinkling stars – he had spelled them all, with one tiny gesture.

Colette thinned her lips. The stars jangled in her head, like the little flashing lights she saw sometimes if she pressed her hands against her eyes. She swept her hand back across the ribbon, calling the magic out of the threads, and curled her fist. She could feel Rizzo's spell, buzzing sharply against her skin. It stabbed her with the points of a hundred tiny constellations.

Colette didn't decide to throw the magic back at

him – her hand simply seemed to move, her fingers flinging the tangled spell without her telling them.

Myriad points of light shimmered in the air, and then sank into Rizzo's skin, leaving him glittering, stars spattered across his face like freckles.

'You idiot!' he snarled. 'That could have been my eye! You could have blinded me.'

'Don't ever interfere in my magic again,' Colette told him coldly. 'I learned that spell yesterday. I haven't spent years practising charms, or reciting magic words, or learning lists of magical herbs or whatever it is you do. *I don't know how it works.* If you do something stupid like messing with my ribbons, I just can't be held responsible for what happens, can I?' She smiled at him, very sweetly, and blew a stray star off the end of the ribbon, so that it hung, sparkling, in the air between them.

He glared at her, and then scratched furiously at his cheeks, leaving tiny red specks where the stars had been. Colette watched him stalk out of the workroom and sighed. She pinched the star out of the air, and pressed it gently into the arm of her chair, to remind her. She had known from the start that he didn't like her but, until now, she hadn't realised how quite how much she hated him.

Colette sat by the canal, staring into the oily darkness of the water. It seemed thick, almost soupy. Nothing like the blue silk – *That was seawater*, she thought dreamily, *far out from land under a heavy summer sky*. Or perhaps the shallows around an island, the way she might have seen it if she had run away to the lacemakers on Burano after all. The canal waters swirled and sucked at the steps below her feet, and Colette pulled back her pretty red leather slippers. They were a present from her father, along with a length of good wool fabric, and one of linen, from which to make herself two new dresses. She had never had such nice shoes. Never. Or such good food, or a room of her own.

But even with her own beautiful room, a settled home in the maskmaker's house, and her own work to do, Colette still didn't feel at home. It didn't matter that she was with her father and Rizzo almost all the day: the apprentice smirked and grimaced at her whenever he could, and her father hardly seemed to notice that she was there. Maria and Lina hadn't the time to talk to her, and the shop clerks had heard all about the master's brat of a daughter from Rizzo, and didn't want anything to do with her.

Colette brushed angrily at her stinging eyes. She wouldn't cry – what if one of them saw her? The maids or, even worse, Rizzo?

A gondola slid by, like a patch of darker shadow on the water, the gondolier poling the boat along with scarcely a splash. A faint ripple sent the water lapping thickly at the steps again, and Colette rested her chin on her knees. What was she going to do? In some ways, she was better off than she had been when living with Ma but, given the choice, she would have gone back to her old life in the time it took to set one stitch. *Perhaps when I'm older, Father will let me set up my own dressmaking establishment,*

Colette thought gloomily. *Father* – that didn't even sound right. She hadn't called him that, not yet. She didn't call him anything, except sir, as Rizzo did, and that only occasionally. She didn't think he noticed, either.

A faint bump sounded, further along the bank, and Colette glanced sideways in surprise. She hadn't heard another boat coming. Whoever it was rowing had been remarkably quiet.

There was no boat.

Colette drew in her feet again, and sat up, ready to whirl around and dash back down the alley to the well-lit square. There was only one dim torch down here, set out by the owners of a house a little way down the waterside. She had been enjoying the dark; it all fitted her miserable mood: the lapping of the water, wheezing creaks from the wooden jetties, and the occasional low murmur from a passing gondola. That damp bumping noise had not fitted in. It was different, and strangely nasty, even though she couldn't work out what it was.

It came again, and Colette caught her breath, trying to tell where the sound was coming from. Somewhere to her right – that rickety wooden jetty, with the rowing boat tied up against it. Perhaps it had just been the boat, caught in the current and swinging against a post? But as the sound came again, Colette knew it wasn't.

She got to her feet, preparing to tiptoe as far as the mouth of the alley, and then she would run. She had taken her first step, blessing the soft leather soles of her new shoes, when the sound came again. A sodden bumping scrabble, but this time, with it, a faint, despairing mew.

Colette turned back. It was a sack – a wet, heavy sack, thumping against the jetty. And she had heard that sound before. Even Ma, who thought cats were a nuisance, had been moved to tears finding a sack of poor drowned kittens caught up under the bridge. Colette shuddered as she hurried down the frail jetty, remembering that moment a few months before, the way the wet fur had been slicked close to the skinny little bodies. But these kittens were still alive – one of them at least.

She knelt on the slippery boards, reaching down into the chill water to haul up the dripping sack. It was caught somehow, the threads looped up on a splinter in the post, and she struggled with it, muttering to herself, 'Please not again. Be alive. It's coming, I'll have you out in a moment, oh please...' Then at last she yanked the heavy bundle out, and laid it streaming on the jetty so she could fight at the clumsy knot in the top. Her fingers were so chilled from the water she could hardly pull the heavy stuff apart. But at last she dragged open the top of the sack, and sat back, fearful of what she might see.

There had been no sound from inside, not since she had pulled it out of the water. Colette sat staring at the unmoving lump, and thought to herself, had she only imagined that mewing? Was the sack empty, after all – was its weight only water? And then a dark, thin paw reached out, and a thin wedge-shaped head, ears laid back. The cat shook itself free of the sack, and stared at Colette. Not a kitten – a fully-grown cat. Black, she thought, though she could hardly see. Perhaps with some grey patches.

'What did you do to offend someone, then?' she murmured. It wasn't that unusual to drown kittens – even if a valued mouser had a litter, her owners might well want to be rid of the little nuisances – but who would bother drowning a grown cat, unless it was for sport? 'Probably it was that Rizzo, and a gang of his apprentice mates,' Colette growled. She'd never seen him be cruel to a cat, but it was the way she felt about him just then. 'Should you like some scraps, cat? A little meat from the kitchen?'

The cat had sat down by the sack, licking its paws and drawing them over its ears. It seemed odd, to want to make itself even wetter, but then, cats always did seem to be washing. Now it stopped mid-swipe, and peered at her – almost as if it had understood, and wanted to know if she could be trusted.

'It'll only be what I can find,' she warned it. In the darkness, it didn't seem so odd to be talking to the creature. 'I can't promise. And if Maria's still in the kitchen, who knows if she'll give me anything. But I can only try. Are you coming, then?' She walked a little way down the jetty, looking back to watch, and felt absurdly pleased when a thin dark shadow padded after her.

As they came towards the end of the alleyway, into the lights from the shops and the church, Colette looked curiously down at the cat, who was now pacing by her side. He wasn't black, as she'd first thought. Or at least, not all over. He was dark, but with gingery patches. Most of his face was the same ginger colour, with dark mask-markings round his golden eyes. They gleamed in the lamplight as Colette stared down at his whiskers – black on one side, white on the other.

'It's you!' she whispered, crouching down to see closer.

The cat gazed back at her, face to face. He didn't run, or even look away; he kept his great golden eyes fixed on Colette's.

'Who tried to drown *you*?' Colette wondered. 'And how did you end up here, just where I'd find you?' She frowned. 'I suppose it isn't so very far away. If someone put you in near Ma's shop, and the tide washed you out into the Grand Canal, there's no reason you shouldn't end up here. Unless I was right, and it was those apprentice friends of Rizzo's. Did you follow me here, cat? And then you fell foul of those beasts?' The cat simply stared at her, and Colette sighed. 'However it happened, it does seem as though I was meant to find you.'

The cat leaned forward and, quite deliberately, nudged his patched face against her cheek. Colette chuckled. 'Was that thank you? Or is it just that I promised you food?' She felt strangely lighter inside. Just seeing the speckled cat had reminded her of home, and Ma. She felt as though a piece of home had come to find her. 'You listened to me once before,' Colette murmured to the cat. 'I told you I thought she was ill. Well, I was quite right, cat. And you were right too, about the countess. I'm so glad I told her I wouldn't go to be her maid. Though mind you' – she glanced over at the maskmaker's shop, on the other side of the little piazza – 'maybe at her palazzo someone might talk to me.' She sighed. 'It's an odd place, that shop. The masks give me shivers. But you'd fit in.' She eyed him cautiously, and put out a hand to stroke the dark fur around his eyes. 'You've got a perfect mask – and I don't mind yours. You're not hiding anything behind it, are you?'

The cat rubbed his face against her hand, and purred a little.

'It's very handsome, your mask,' Colette told him comfortingly, as she ran her hand on down his back. 'Oh, you're still so wet! I forgot!' Without thinking, she scooped him up in her arms, and ran across the piazza. The cat sat rigid in her arms, and Colette glanced down at him anxiously, wondering if he'd dart away. He was a stray, after all, and no one's pet. He wasn't used to being carried. But he didn't squirm, although Colette thought perhaps he wanted to.

She made for the little side door, not the grand

glass-paned entry to the shop, and slipped inside, realising how lucky she was that her father hadn't locked it up. She had no idea what time it was, but it felt as though she had been sitting by the water for an hour or more.

Colette crept through the house, making for the kitchens at the back. In the candlelight, she could see the cat peering curiously around, his ears flicking back and forth. She wondered how many times he'd been inside a house – Ma had chased him out in seconds, when he'd sneaked in. He was probably used to sleeping under bridges. 'Do you like it?' she whispered to him, pausing by the open door into the shop. The masks glimmered faintly in the light from the passageway, and Colette drew back again. 'I don't. But I don't think I have a choice, not like you. I suppose I could run away, but I'm not really brave enough. Not yet, anyway. This is the kitchen, look. Oh, the lamp is out. Maria and Lina must have gone to bed.' She poked a taper into the embers of the fire, and relit the lamp, holding it up to look around. 'I've hardly been in here,' she explained to the cat. 'I suppose there must be a larder… I've never seen so much food as my father eats – meat at every meal!' She pulled open a small wooden door, and smiled at the sight of the larder: rows of bottles and crocks and jars, all lined up on solid stone shelves. The jars glinted in the lamplight, just as the masks had, but they glowed with the rich jewel colours of bottled fruit and cordials and preserves.

'Sardines, look,' Colette whispered to the cat. He had his front paws up on the lowest shelf, sniffing urgently at the rows of jars. A tiny, dust-brown mouse streaked out from behind a jar of preserved peaches, and disappeared into the shadows of the kitchen. The cat eyed it smugly, and then nudged Colette's hand, as though reminding her what she was supposed to be doing.

'Yes…ugh. Though I suppose we shouldn't be here, either. Anyway, look. Sardines – you'll like these. They're my father's favourite, preserved in oil and vinegar. He had them for dinner.'

The cat was purring now, twisting himself around and about her legs, purring so hard she could feel him trembling against her dress. Colette tipped out two fat sardines onto the lid of the crock and carried them into the kitchen, with the cat leaping around her all the way. She set the lid down by the fire and watched the cat gulping at the fish, swallowing down the chunks so hungrily that his whole body jumped and shook. The sardines were gone in a few seconds, then he scoured the lid clean with his tongue, working all round in case he'd left a drop of oil. Then he gave it one last suspicious sniff, obviously checking it for any tang of leftover fish, but he was forced to admit that he'd eaten every bit. He sat down by the fire, looking pleased with himself, and swiped his paws thoroughly over his greasy whiskers.

'So that was good, then…' Colette murmured. 'What shall we do, cat? Are you staying? I should go upstairs, it's late. You could come with me…?' She looked at him doubtfully. He seemed such a wild, singular sort of creature. Would he want to become a house pet? Would he sleep on a bed? Perhaps he wouldn't even want to go upstairs.

But the cat followed her up the stairs curiously, and he turned out to be quite intrigued by the bed. He sniffed the extravagant fronds of embroidery on her coverlet quite as thoroughly as he'd inspected the fish-flavoured lid. Then he hooked one lethal, pearl-grey claw into a clump of threads, tugging at them gently. He didn't rip the embroidery, even though Colette was sure he could have done if he'd tried. It was as if he could sense the magic, and he found it curious. He kept looking from her to the embroidery and back again, his yellow-green eyes brighter and rounder than ever.

'I didn't actually mean to,' Colette admitted, sitting down next to him, and tracing the pattern of the embroidery with one finger. 'It was just such boring, everyday work, and I could see how much nicer it could have been.' She smiled as she felt the threads stir a little under her touch. The cat crouched low, his skinny shoulder blades rising up through his dappled fur, and peered at the stitches, fascinated.

Then he sniffed dismissively, turned so that he was sitting, and began to wash the backs of his legs, sticking them straight up in the air in a rather undignified position.

Colette felt quite gratified. He wasn't put off by her magic. Quite the opposite – surely washing like that meant that he was settled, and comfortable? Perhaps even slightly *too* comfortable. But there was no denying that, right at that moment, she hardly felt lonely at all.

When Colette woke the next morning, the cat was sitting on her windowsill, next to the open window. He was staring out into the drizzle, but when he saw that she was awake, he leaped onto the bed, and came stalking up the coverlet, purring loudly and butting his head against her hands. His fur was slightly damp, Colette noticed, and there were faint greyish pawprints on the coverlet – little muddy marks that stayed for a second and then seemed to be sucked down inside the fabric. 'Oh, you are clever,' she murmured. 'You went out of the window. So you are house-trained, after all. I was worried. I don't think Maria and Lina would be keen on my keeping you if you weren't.'

The cat looked meaningfully towards the bedroom door, and Colette got out of bed. 'Yes. Breakfast. And perhaps it would be better to go downstairs and mention you to my father, *before* Maria comes to wake me.'

The cat flowed gracefully down the stairs in front of Colette, while she dashed after him, hoping that they wouldn't run into anyone before she'd explained. Even just two fat sardines seemed to have given the cat's fur a shine it hadn't had before. He looked bigger too, even though she was sure he couldn't be. *Perhaps it's just because he isn't cringing under a bridge...*

Her father opened the workroom door as Colette passed on the way to the parlour, and she jumped. Had he been working in there all night? His clothes were rumpled – and that was yesterday's shirt, she was sure. The apprentice appeared behind him, pale and yawning.

'Ah! Colette, my dear.' Her father patted her cheek. 'Is it breakfast? I seem to have lost track of time. But we have done excellent work.' He looked back briefly, over his shoulder. 'Rizzo, not long for breakfast. We shall lose the thread.'

Rizzo glanced at him resentfully, and for once Colette felt sorry for the boy. She supposed that if his master wanted to work through the night without sleep, he had to as well. 'There's a cat,' he muttered, pointing, and Colette lost all her sympathy at once. She meant to have introduced the subject gradually.

'Chase it out, Rizzo,' her father waved at the cat vaguely. 'Remember that great white beast that came in through the workshop window and tangled itself in the spells? Better not let this one do the same.'

'He's my cat!' Colette broke in, stepping in front of Rizzo. She even pressed her hands against his waistcoat, and the boy stared down at her in shock. 'I mean, he followed me from Ma's house. I think. But someone tried to drown him in the canal, in a sack. He's very good. He'll chase the mice out of the workshop. Don't they nibble at the spells?'

'Come here, cat.' Her father used the same voice he had to get her out from behind the door, and the cat seemed to know he was being enchanted, just as Colette had. Each step he took was slow and unwilling as the magic dragged him forward, and all the hair had risen up along his spine. His tail had swelled to twice its usual size.

'He's not a very beautiful beast, Colette.' Her father glanced at her. 'Wouldn't you rather have a little dog to sit in your lap?'

'No!' Colette shuddered. She was no fine lady, to have of those spoiled, yappy little creatures. 'No, sir. A useful mouser, that's what we need.'

'Mmm. Well, if he disturbs the spells, he goes. But you may keep him.' He rubbed a hand over the cat's ears, and golden sparks fizzed along the ends of the sticking-up fur. 'Beautiful or no, Colette, now I look at him, he's most suitable for a maskmaker's workshop. Look at his masked face.'

'I know,' Colette admitted. 'It's very striking. Perhaps he'll be more beautiful when he's better fed, sir.'

Rizzo's stomach rumbled, and the cat's ears pricked up. The maskmaker laughed, and nodded. 'Tell Maria to bring the breakfast,' he said, waving Colette to the stairs. 'She can bring the masked cat a dish of his own. You should name him that, Colette. *Il Mascherato*.'

'Sir.' One of the shop clerks peered apologetically around the workshop door. Only his nose showed, as though he wanted to be able to duck back quickly, in case anything was thrown at him. 'Sir, the Countess Morezzi is here. She wants to discuss a new commission, sir, and she won't speak to me, or Nicolo.'

'Curse the woman,' Colette's father muttered. 'She would. Just now, when it's going so well.'

Colette realised that she had crushed the black

ribbons she was embroidering between her fingers. Carefully, she unclenched her hands, and flattened out the crumpled embroidery. The ribbons were for cat masks – very popular with young girls, her father said. It had taken Colette several weeks of work to finish the starry ribbon to his satisfaction – she had unpicked the spells so many times to make them perfect that by the time she had finished, there was hardly anything of the original ribbon left underneath the layers of magic. But her magic had grown stronger every time.

She had been resentful, the first time her father had shaken his head and suggested that she should try again, but she had grown to love the pattern of stars, and all the little intricacies she had stitched into it along the way.

Now Signor Sorani had allowed Colette to devise her own design, and she was working on a spell that made the hundred tiny green cats' eyes blink open and closed.

The masked cat – Colette had shortened

Il Mascherato to 'Max' – had been perched on the arm of her chair, staring intently at them. Now he looked at her, and blinked his own green-gold eyes, very slowly, as though asking her what she thought she was doing.

'You know her,' Colette whispered to him. She wasn't really convinced that he could understand her, but he looked as though he did, and it was comforting to have someone to talk to. 'The countess – she's the one who kicked you. But that was weeks and weeks ago. You probably don't remember.'

Max's whiskers shook, and he let out a faint hiss. Colette nodded. 'Exactly. You do remember her, then. Do you think we should go downstairs too?'

Her father was taking off his apron and the gauntlets he wore for certain dangerous magics. Rizzo fetched his braided coat from a hook behind the door, and he shrugged it on with a sigh. The pair of them set off downstairs, without a word to Colette. It was this that decided her. After all, could her father not have said something? He knew that the countess had met her, and even offered Colette a position in her household. He could have told her not to let herself be seen. Instead, he seemed to have forgotten she was there – again. Colette was sick of being forgotten. She would go downstairs, and see.

Colette and Max tiptoed down the stairs after the others and stood by the open door that led from the main house into the shop. The countess was sitting on a small gilded chair, with the same bored-looking page in attendance. The two clerks were lurking behind the counter, obviously intending to stay out of the way; Rizzo looked as though he wished he could join them.

Colette's father was standing in front of the countess, stroking his chin in such a studied way that Colette wanted to laugh. It was his 'thoughtful artist' pose. She suspected that actually he was trying to work out what he could get away with charging the countess.

'I need something a little...special,' the countess

murmured. 'You know what I mean, dearest Signor Sorani.'

Colette flinched, remembering the sharp, demanding way the countess had always spoken to her mother – as if she had been less than a servant, even. *Our dresses were just as beautiful as his masks*, she thought angrily to herself.

'Something to further enhance my lady's exquisite beauty…'

Colette shuddered as her father bowed low. His voice was as sweet as syrup.

'Well, of course… Your previous work has indeed been effective,' the countess purred back, laying a slim white hand on his arm. 'But I need something a little different this time. Stronger. I need people to *understand* me, Signor Sorani. I need to be…more persuasive, shall we say?'

Colette heard Rizzo catch his breath, and the countess's shoulders stiffened slightly. She didn't say anything – of course she would not take notice of a mere apprentice – but the very air inside the room seemed chillier. It was quite impressive to be able to do that without magic, Colette realised. That was pure willpower.

Her father changed position slightly, shielding the countess from his unruly apprentice. Or perhaps the other way around.

'I see. You do understand, my lady, that such a thing would require a great many enchantments? They would have to be woven into the very paper from which we create the masks. It would not be a case of simply laying a spell over the top.'

Colette bit her lip. So he would do it, then? If the countess paid him enough, her father would make her a mask that made it impossible to disobey her? For that was what she meant, however she dressed it up.

'Of course.' The countess nodded. 'You mean to say that it will be very expensive.' She smiled at him, showing very good teeth – *Which are probably as false as the rest of her*, Colette decided grimly. She peered a little further around the door.

'I am afraid so, my lady. And also time consuming. My time is a little shorter, lately, my lady. My young daughter has come to live with me, and I must assume charge of her education. I believe you have met her, strangely enough, at her mother's establishment.'

Colette froze. She felt Max pressing against her ankles, and longed to pick him up, but she couldn't move.

'Colette, come and be introduced to Countess Morezzi,' her father called. He hadn't even looked around. *But then any magician of his skill would know who was lurking behind him*, Colette thought bitterly. Of course he would. 'Stay there!' she whispered to Max. The countess would be annoyed enough as it was.

She slipped through the door, and curtseyed deeply to the countess, grateful for the new clothes her father had provided for her. The richer fabrics made her feel stronger, when faced with a noble lady dressed in pearl-embroidered satin. 'My lady,' she murmured.

'The seamstress's child… She's *your* daughter?

How very amusing.' But the countess did not sound amused at all. 'And is she helping in your shop now, Signor Sorani? She embroiders most exquisitely.'

'Indeed she does. Colette is furthering her magical education by embroidering ribbons for our masks, my lady. I'm sure she will be delighted to work out a new design for your commission.'

I most certainly won't, Colette said to herself. Wasn't it enough that the countess had both noble birth *and* money? How could it be fair to make her irresistible as well?

But her father was bowing low, ushering the countess out of the shop with many promises of his finest work, his strongest spells – everything to be just as 'my lady' wanted.

'How could you?' Colette hissed as soon as she'd left the shop. 'She's a monster! You said so yourself – that she wants to steal magic for her own, to make her even more powerful. How could you agree to make her something like that? No one will be able to stand up against her at all!'

Her father grabbed her by the arm, and herded her and Rizzo back up the stairs to the workroom. 'A little sense, Colette,' he muttered, as he leaned back against the closed door. 'Not where the boys can hear us. Did you not notice how very careful the countess and I were to skirt around what she was actually asking for?'

'You shouldn't have been,' Colette snapped back. 'You should have just said no.'

'You do realise that her husband is part of the duchess's council, don't you?' her father pointed out, wearily tucking the lace cuffs of his shirt up into his sleeves again, and pulling on his apron. 'One doesn't *just* say *no* to a Morezzi.'

'But then what are you going to do?' Colette asked, sitting down limply by her sewing table.

'I really don't know, dear heart,' her father muttered. 'I don't know at all.'

Chapter Seven

Over the next few weeks, Colette's father began work on the new mask. He had sent a message to the countess, telling her how difficult her project was, and that it could take him some months to work out the spells he would need. He asked if perhaps she would like to cancel her commission. But she sent back the answer no. She was sure that dear Signor Sorani would produce the mask eventually. She was happy to wait – however long it took.

Colette watched her father frowning over the

message that night, and she read it herself later on, since he'd left it lying on the workbench. It sounded like a threat, to her. Veiled, to be sure, but definitely there.

'I must do it,' he told Colette, when she saw him setting out his tools and his drawings for the new mask. She had tried to argue with him again, but he only laughed at her – a strange, bitter, sad laugh.

'I can't not, Colette. You must be one of the few people to defy the Countess Morezzi and not end up regretting it. She could ruin my business. If her husband brought the power of the duchess's council against me, he could have the shop closed down.'

'He couldn't...' Colette looked at him doubtfully.

'Of course he could! He's one of Duchess Olivia's closest advisors. From all I've heard, he's a good man. Solid. Honest. But his wife...'

'I suppose I didn't matter enough for her to want to punish me,' Colette murmured. Somehow it was hard to think of Countess Morezzi – or her husband – as part of the duchess's court. Ma had always admired the Little Duchess, and taught Colette to do the same. She'd told Colette stories of the duchess's kindness, and her charity, and her sweetness to the Lady Mia. Even though she profoundly distrusted magic, Ma hadn't minded it in the duchess. After all, her magic was part of Venice, it ran through the water, and deep into the salt marshes under the city. She *had* to be magical for the city to survive. Her magic was nothing like the countess's greedy desires.

'Or she's biding her time. I didn't know whether to tell her you were here, Colette, but I decided in the end that since she's so desperate for this mask, she wouldn't do anything to upset me. Not at the moment, anyway. It seemed better to tell the truth now, instead of later.' He sighed, and pressed his fingers hard against his temples, as though he had a headache. 'And now, of course, it's not only the shop she could take away from me.'

Colette looked at him blankly. 'Why, what else is there?'

Her father lifted up his head and stared at her.

'You, Colette! She can take you!'

'Oh.' Colette sat down rather limply on one of the stools. 'Yes, I see. I suppose she thinks you'd mind.'

'I would mind!'

Colette frowned at him in surprise. 'Would you really?'

'You are the strangest child,' her father muttered. 'Yes, Colette, I would. Not only do you remind me of your mother – who was the love of my life, even if we couldn't be in the same room for half an hour without fighting – but you are my daughter. My own flesh and blood. How can you not know that I'd do anything to keep you safe?'

'You've only known me for a few weeks!' Colette retorted. *And an awful lot of that time you've hardly noticed I was here…* she added silently.

'It makes no difference.' He shook his head. 'Always know that I will protect you, Colette – but that makes you valuable, to someone like Countess Morezzi. Be careful.' He kissed her cheek. 'Go up to bed, child. I want no one else here, while I work on this...thing. I have sent Rizzo out to carouse with those no-good apprentice boys. Neither of you should see the kind of magic I will have to use.'

From then on, he worked on the mask every night, after the day's other business was done, and always alone. Colette was sure that he was growing paler and more tired after each night's work, but he refused to take a night away from the new mask, even though she begged. For once, Rizzo agreed with her.

'She's right,' he muttered, after Colette's father had smilingly told her not to fuss. 'You look ill, sir. You've been working late into the night for a fortnight now. You're pale, and there are great shadows under your eyes. That mask is draining the power out of you.' He shuddered, and glanced towards the countess's mask, where it hung on the wall, waiting for its next night of spells. It was such a pretty thing, silvery and delicate; it didn't look as though it could drain the power out of a master magician. But Colette hated to pass the point on the wall where it hung –

even just walking by, she could feel the dark hunger inside the mask, the way it dragged at her magic, drawing her close. She would find her lips twisting in a faint, foolish smile, and her feet would tap, as if the mask wanted her to dance. And then she'd tear herself out of its clutches, cursing, and the mask's dark eye-hollows would follow her as she pulled away. It twinkled, and laughed, and she was sure it tucked away each little wisp of magic that it stole, somewhere safe.

Colette's father would not be persuaded. Each night he took down the mask, reaching up to unhook it with a pained, almost frightened expression on his face. Then he would dismiss Rizzo and Colette, and they heard him muttering spells as they went up the stairs to their rooms.

'Sir, these are all dry.' Rizzo turned around on the ladder, looking down at Colette's father. He was inspecting the papier-mâché masks that they had made a few days before and hung up on the wooden drying frame in the corner of the workroom. 'Shall I bring them down? Do you want to see if any of them are good enough to use?'

There was a moment of expectant silence, and Colette looked up from her sewing just as Rizzo added sharply, 'Sir!' He had enough magic to add a spell to the words, making it almost impossible for Colette's father to ignore him.

There was a ringing clatter as the silver mask fell from Signor Sorani's hands onto the workbench, and Colette swallowed painfully as she watched his face. It was dead white, making the dark circles under his eyes stand out like some strange carnival make-up.

'You were about to put it on,' Rizzo hissed. 'Sir, you never put them on, never.'

'No, no...' Colette's father murmured. 'Why would I put it on? I'm not making it for myself, boy, am I?'

'But you were! You had it up to your face,' Rizzo protested. 'How can you not remember...?' His voice shook and died, and he turned back to the ghostlike paper masks on the drying frame, gathering them up with trembling hands.

'Yes, yes, bring them down,' Signor Sorani muttered impatiently. He hung the silver mask back on the wall, but Colette could see the way his hands lingered caressingly before he turned away.

Rizzo was right – if he hadn't shouted, her father would have put on the mask.

Colette wasn't sure what would have happened then. It was hard enough for her even walking past the thing; she couldn't imagine what would happen if it were actually touching her, pressed up against her skin, her eyes. She would never, never be able to take it off. But her father had created the mask – surely that would mean it was under his control, wouldn't it?

She watched as Rizzo descended the ladder, the pile of masks clattering together as his hands shook. Rizzo knew a lot more about masks than she did – and their power. For once, Colette actually wished that she could talk to him.

That night, neither Colette nor Rizzo tried to persuade Signor Sorani to sleep. It was obvious now that he could no more leave the mask alone than he could leave off breathing. He had spent that whole day caressing it, wandering away from his workbench to look deep into the dark holes that were its eyes.

Max had followed her out of the workroom, but as she shut the door, he mewed, and stood up, batting against the wooden panels with his speckled paws.

'What is it?' Colette asked, crouching down next to him. 'A mouse?'

But Max stared at her, round-eyed, and leaned closer to the door. Colette pressed her ear against the wood and heard a voice. Her father, of course. He quite often muttered to himself while he was working – and he spoke the spells aloud, sometimes.

'I know,' she murmured. 'He's working on the mask. I don't like it either, but I can't stop him.' She sighed, and stroked Max's ears, rubbing the thin silkiness between her fingers. Then she gasped, and jumped back, cradling her hand, the pale skin marked with four red spots, the points of the cat's sharpest teeth. Max had *bitten* her. He had never done that before. He had never even scratched – the only time he even pricked her was when he insisted on lying on her feet and kneading his paws. He couldn't be made to understand that claws were sharp.

Colette stared at him in dismay as the cat hissed crossly, and caught the lace frill around her elbow in his teeth, pulling her back towards the door.

He was staring at her so meaningfully that Colette leaned her face against the crack where the door met the frame, and tried to listen.

At first, she could only hear her father – but he didn't seem to be repeating a spell, or muttering, the way he did when he was thinking something through. It sounded more as though he was answering a question.

'But there's no one in there with him,' Colette whispered. And then, 'Sorry,' when Max drew back his muzzle in a angry hiss. She listened again, and then a chill ran down the back of her neck, like a little droplet of cold water sliding over her skin.

A thin, light voice was speaking inside the room. Colette couldn't make out the words – they came from over on the other side of the room – but it sounded as if the voice was delivering instructions. It was not her father – even if he had been putting on a different voice, he could never sound like that. And there was no one else in the room. It was just her father and the mask.

Colette pressed her hand against her mouth, fighting against a sudden wave of faintness. That silvery voice sickened her. She scooped up Max and ran for the refuge of her room, to huddle under the wild embroideries and pretend that she was safe.

'It was talking to him, wasn't it?' Colette murmured to Max, when at last she dared to crawl out from under the covers. 'Oh, wake up and listen!' The cat was curled up next to her on the bed, with one paw snuggled over his eyes. Colette was sure that he was only pretending to be asleep. 'I still don't know what we should do. I'm afraid of that mask. It drags at me…' She swallowed. 'Perhaps we ought to get rid of it? What would happen if I cut it up? I could, I'm sure, if I tried hard enough. It's only paper under all that paint, after all.'

Max opened the one eye that she could almost see under his paw. A glint of green shone out at her for a moment, and then flicked shut, and Colette sighed. 'I don't know what that means! Yes, it's a good idea? Or don't be so stupid? I do wish you could talk, cat. But I can't see anything else that we can do, and we surely must do something.' She nodded her head determinedly. 'I shall steal the mask, and destroy it. If I can't rip it up, I'll throw it in the canal, and all its glue will melt away.' She shivered. 'I don't know what it will try to do back to me. Or what the countess will say, or my father. But I must.' She clasped her hands around her knees, and rested her chin on top, gazing into the shadows. 'My father often finishes his magic in the early hours,' she murmured. 'I have heard him, I'm sure, coming up the stairs, just as the sky is growing light. Once he is safely in his chamber, I shall hurry down to the workroom, and steal that mask.'

The cat woke up properly this time. He sat sphinx-like on the bed, his paws stretched out in front, and gazed seriously at Colette. 'I know,' she muttered. 'But it's only a mask. I don't see how it can be that dangerous – I mean, it can't control me unless I put it on, can it? And of course I'm not going to do that. That's where I have the advantage over my father. I've hated masks for so long, I'd never, ever put one on.' She looked down, plucking at the threads of the embroidery on her bedcover. 'I need to wake up when it gets light,' she murmured, teasing out a strand of pale pink thread. 'When the sky is this colour – and this – and this.' She twisted the pink thread with a lilac one, and a golden yellow. 'Then I'll wake up.'

Max leaned over to look at the new pattern of the threads – a tiny patch of pink sky, streaked with lilac, the first faint rays of sun flooding out across the clouds. He sniffed at it, and sneezed, and sat back looking affronted.

'Does it smell too sharp?' Colette teased him. 'Don't you like the smell of magic? You have to, in this house.' Then she shivered, and curled herself up into a ball. 'Or perhaps it's just dangerous magic you don't like. But I don't have a choice.' She hauled the covers up around her ears, so that the sky patch was pressed against her cheek, and closed her eyes determinedly, repeating the sleep charm that all the mothers in her quarter had hushed their children with.

The sea will send a dark ship to carry my nightmares away,

But my dreams will float upon the quiet waters until morning.

Colette rolled over with a groan, burying her head under the covers to shut out the sun. But the light was too bright – it even came through the fabric. And she could feel Max walking up and down on her back.

Jumping, it felt like. Growling, she wriggled out from underneath the coverlet, and stared at the sunshine shining out of her embroidery.

The rest of the room was quite dark still – there was just a faint, pearly light coming in through the window. Only the tiny piece of sky she had created was shining. Colette's lips twisted in a smile, just for a second. A month or so before, she would never have believed that she could sew a sky. She had thought all this time that she wanted to go back to Ma's shop, and the safety of stitching dresses. But now she was sure that she could never give up the magic. 'I'd rather have the magic without the soul-eating masks, mind you,' she whispered to herself. 'I suppose I should get out of bed.'

Max put one paw on top of the sky-threads, and watched rather gloomily as the light flooded out around his pads.

'I know. I don't actually want to, either. Not now that it's now.' Colette got up, and hurriedly pulled on a shift, and her old skirt and bodice – they were easier and quicker to do up than her new clothes, which were designed for a girl who had maids to help her. Then she opened her door, lifting up the latch in fractions so as not to let it creak.

She padded along the landing, stopping to listen outside her father's door. Was he upstairs already?

Max stood up on his hind legs again, and pushed the door with his paws so that it ghosted open. Colette could see her father, collapsed fully dressed on the bed. She bit her lip – he looked so exhausted. In the dawn light, his face seemed made of shadows, and he looked years older than he had when she had first met him a month before. His hair was speckled with glittering white threads among the black.

'Let's go,' she whispered to Max. Colette had been wavering, but after seeing her father so broken, she fought down her fear of the mask.

They hurried down the stairs to the workroom, and Colette marched in, refusing to look at the mask until she'd unlatched the heavy shutters, letting the pale sun creep into the room.

The masks looked smaller in the daylight, and Colette drew in a breath of relief as she turned. They were just paper. Without the flickering candlelight, their eyeholes didn't seem to follow her any more.

She clenched her teeth tightly together and stared determinedly at the countess's mask. Even in the morning light, it somehow kept the pools of dark shadow inside its eye sockets. As she reached up to unhook it from the wall, the air around the mask seemed to move, as if the mask were breathing. Colette shuddered as the breath rolled over her, heavy with spells. It felt like a warning. She closed her eyes and stretched determinedly forwards, feeling the smooth surface of the mask. Her father was an expert craftsman – the mask was perfect. As she lifted it, it seemed to soften against her hands, becoming warm, pliable – almost skin-like.

Colette began to wonder what it would feel like if she put it on. She had never wanted to wear a mask, but this one – this one was special.

It was too dangerous, of course. She mustn't raise

it to her face. It couldn't work any magic unless someone was wearing it, surely – she knew that. So that meant it would be stupid to put it on.

But it was so warm, so invitingly soft.

Could it really do any harm, just to try it for a moment? She would glance at herself in the mirror, and then take it off. She had to take it off, because there was something she was supposed to do with the mask, although she couldn't quite remember what... She'd probably remember what it was she had to do when she'd put the mask on, Colette thought, smiling, as she lifted it towards her face. The mask would help her remember. It was so clever, and so beautiful. She could feel how special and clever it was, now that she was holding it up to her face.

A sudden burning pain streaked across Colette's hand, and she gasped. The mask was torn out of her fingers as she reeled against the workbench, feeling sick.

'What happened?' she whispered, looking down at Max. His fur was all on end, his tail fluffed up to twice its usual size. He was crouched in front of the mask, hissing furiously.

'Did you knock it out of my hands?' Colette asked, sliding down to sit next to him on the floor, nursing the deep scratches across the back of her hand.

Max nudged his face against her skirt, his fur settling a little. 'Yes,' he murmured. 'It was glowing, and your eyes had changed – they were black, like the holes in the mask, and that was even before you had actually put it on.'

Colette pulled back the hand that was reaching out to stroke him, and stared. Perhaps she had hit her head on the bench as she went down. She blinked a few times, and shook her head gently. It didn't hurt.

'What are you doing?' Max sniffed at her hair. 'Are you hurt?'

'No.' Colette looked into his eyes. 'You actually are talking, aren't you? I'm not just making it up?'

The cat skittered back, staring at her, his ears laid back. 'No!' He sat down under the workbench and started to wash his ragged ears, still darting suspicious glances at Colette in between swipes of his paw. 'Stupid girl. Talking! Cats don't talk to humans, do they?'

'But you are,' Colette insisted. 'I can hear you! How could I be answering your question if I hadn't heard what you said?'

'I don't know! Perhaps you're just guessing.'

'I'm not guessing – how could I guess you'd just said that?' Colette crawled under the bench next to him, and Max glared at her suspiciously. She stared into his golden eyes, her heart thudding. This was stranger even than her own growing magic. 'Maybe you're not actually talking out loud – it's just that now I can understand what you've always been saying?'

'Perhaps,' the cat admitted reluctantly.

'You could try talking to Rizzo, or the maids, and see if they can hear you. Maybe it'll sound just like purring or mewing to them?'

'I don't particularly want to talk to you, let alone anyone else,' the cat hissed irritably. Then, after a moment of hurt silence from Colette, he turned his head to look at her. 'All right,' he growled. 'I didn't quite mean that. This is all very surprising. You don't know.' His tail swished from side to side.

Colette stared at her knees. 'I do. It happened to me too, you know. Everything started to move under my fingers. Everything was different.' She ran a cautious hand down the nobbled lumps of his spine. 'You still feel just that same. To me, I mean. Do you' – she swallowed, not wanting to upset him – 'do you suppose you can still talk to other cats?'

Max flattened his ears back. 'I don't know. I wouldn't say that I ever did talk to them. We… exchanged news, I suppose. Who was where. Whose land was whose. That sort of thing. We didn't talk about magic glowing masks,' he added resentfully. 'This is all your fault.'

'You really don't like it?' Colette asked wistfully. 'Talking? Perhaps I could use the mask to take it away again – I mean, it must be because of the mask that it's happened, mustn't it? When you knocked it away from me, that's when this happened. It has to be the mask that did it. You were wanting so much to tell me something that perhaps it gave you the power to talk.' She reached for the mask. 'I suppose it must be able to take it away again. If you really don't want it.'

'Are you mad?' the cat hissed. He swept his tail round in a great arc, sending the mask flying across the room. 'It's still working on you, isn't it? You're not touching that thing again. You were about to put it on before, don't you realise? What do you think it would have done to you? Your father's half enslaved by it as it is! We're not giving the blasted thing your magic too.'

'Is he?' Colette crouched down to look more closely into Max's eyes, but the cat jerked his head away.

'Don't do that, don't stare. And yes. You were right, wanting to destroy it. But as soon as you come close, it will begin to work on you – you'll only remember how beautiful it is, and how clever.'

The cat got up and stalked over to the mask, picking it up in his teeth. Colette saw the fur rise up all along his back, and when he stepped forward, he seemed to be pushing against some invisible force. The mask was fighting him. She hurried closer, watching anxiously as he dragged himself across the room to the wall, dropping the mask just under the empty hook, so it looked as though it might have fallen down. Then he slumped down on the wooden boards, his sides heaving.

Colette scooped him up, hugging him tightly against her chest – he felt loose and saggy, like an old cloth doll, but his eyes glittered with triumph. 'Now we don't have to explain. Ugh, it burns.' He shivered, and leaped down, shaking his ears as if to fling away the taint of the magic. 'Come on. Back upstairs. That thing has your father enslaved. Better to be in your room, all innocent, when it starts to whisper to him about this morning's work.'

Chapter Eight

COLETTE FOLLOWED THE RAGGED CAT back up the stairs, still only half believing that she had heard him speak. Perhaps it was a dream – she was tired enough. Even dragging herself up the steps was an effort, and when she reached the first landing she paused for a moment, staggering against the wall with a thump. Max turned back, flattening his ears in disapproval. ‘Shhh! We’re trying not to wake your father, remember.’

‘I know… I’m sorry. I’m just so tired.’

He padded back and caught her skirt in his teeth, pulling at her gently. 'That mask dragged half your magic out of you. Come on.'

'What are you doing?'

Colette whirled around and almost fell again.

Rizzo was standing in his bedroom doorway, obviously having just scrambled into his breeches and tucked his nightshirt into them. He looked sleepy, but dangerous – he was clutching a candlestick like a weapon. 'Why are you creeping around in the middle of the night?'

'You call this the middle of the night?' Max snapped. 'You don't know you're born.'

There was silence while Colette and Rizzo both turned to stare at him. The cat stared back, and then turned his head sideways, tail twitching. 'I said that out loud.'

'Yes. And I thought you wanted to keep it a secret that you could talk!' Colette frowned at him, and then paused. Perhaps he hadn't said that – perhaps she had wanted it to be their secret. She certainly hadn't wanted to share it with the boy.

'I've only been able to do it for the time it takes to have a really thorough wash,' Max muttered. 'And I don't understand how it works. I could never do it before, and now it seems to be happening all the time. It's confusing! Why are you out here anyway, boy?'

'I heard a noise,' Rizzo said flatly. 'And then people talking. It was too early to be Maria, and who would she be talking to, anyway? How can you talk? Are you the girl's familiar? I never saw you look the least bit magical before.'

Max bridled, swishing his tail. 'All cats are magical, to a certain degree,' he snapped. 'A great deal more than most humans. All that has happened is that now you are able to understand me. I don't know why you're making such a fuss.'

Rizzo opened his mouth and then shut it again a few times, like a fish. Then he obviously gave up on finding anything to say and just stood there, staring at the cat.

'I need to sit down,' Colette said wearily. 'Here,

look.' She perched on the wide stone windowsill, and patted it, inviting Rizzo and Max to sit beside her.

'Are you sick?' Rizzo asked, rather gruffly, as if he didn't really want to be considerate.

'No, it was the mask – Max thinks it drained the magic out of me. We were going to destroy it,' Colette explained. 'It's making my father ill. I was going to tear it up. Or cut it, or something.'

Rizzo snorted.

'What?' Colette glared at him.

'You'd have a job, tearing up any Sorani mask.' He shivered. 'Let alone that one.'

'You've seen it too, then?' Colette asked him eagerly. 'I'm not being silly? It is…working on him.'

'It's working on everybody it can get hold of,' Rizzo growled. 'I don't like being left alone with the thing.' He glanced sideways at her, to check she wasn't laughing. 'It talks to me.'

'We heard it, talking to my father,' Colette agreed. 'It definitely tried to steal my magic out of me. And then when we went to destroy it, I couldn't.

It made me want to put it on.'

'You didn't?' Rizzo demanded anxiously.

'I was going to. I only didn't because Max leaped at me and knocked it out of my hands. And, even then, it was still working on me. I knew it was dangerous, but I still nearly picked it up again. It's as if the mask can see inside us – it sneaks itself into whatever else is happening. It's clever.'

'I keep finding myself standing underneath it and looking at it,' Rizzo admitted. 'I nearly took it off the wall, once, and then you happened to come into the workshop and I realised what I was doing. And then I could hear it hissing at me as I walked away,' he added in a whisper. 'It was angry that I'd escaped.'

'I still don't understand why my father would agree to make such a thing,' Colette said, leaning back against the window and stroking Max. 'He knew it was dangerous – that's why he kept sending us out while he was working on it. Why did he ever say yes to the countess? I don't believe she would have made her husband shut down the shop. He couldn't, could he?'

Rizzo frowned. 'Maybe. Maybe not. But I don't think that was the only reason.' He eyed Colette doubtfully.

'What? Tell me. You can't not...'

'He's in debt. To the countess, or one of her cronies. More than one, actually, I think.'

'But the shop makes lots of money!' Colette protested. 'And his clothes – they're so fancy, and he bought so many things for me too. He can't be in debt!' She shook her head, thinking of the hand-to-mouth life she had lived with Ma, surviving from one dress to the next. 'All the food,' she moaned. 'The waste! And the servants. Is it the rent? But I thought he owned this house?'

'He does,' Rizzo agreed. 'And you're right, the shop makes more money than you could believe, sometimes. But he's spent it. It's not just the clothes and the food, though he is extravagant. He has a habit of going to the Ridotto.' He rolled his eyes as

Colette looked at him, puzzled. 'You know! The casino, the gambling club. In the Palazzo San Moise. Haven't you ever heard of it?'

'Of course I have,' Colette snapped. 'I've just never known anybody who actually went there. What does he do?'

'They all go to play cards. Basetta or Faro mostly.' He sighed at her blank look. 'You don't have any idea what I'm talking about, do you?'

'Good pickings at those clubs,' Max murmured. 'A lot of leftover food. They're all too keen on the cards to bother eating.' His pink tongue shot out for a second, and a faint breath of a purr followed it.

Rizzo nodded. To Colette, he looked as though he was enjoying her ignorance. There was a superior curl to his lip. 'The master went there first to look at the masks,' he explained. 'There are rules at the Ridotto, remember. One must be in evening dress, with a mask, and a tricorne – a three-cornered hat. It was a good place to see what the nobility was wearing. But then it was hard for him to be there and not gamble.

Once he started...he couldn't stop. He lost a lot of money to a Signor Di Mercurio. He is – er—'

Colette decided that Rizzo was probably trying to find a way to describe Signor Di Mercurio without being rude.

'—someone my mother wouldn't have liked me to talk about?' she suggested.

'Yes. And I think Di Mercurio's a card-sharp, as well as everything else. He cheats. And he's a friend of Countess Morezzi.'

Max leaned around to look up at Rizzo. 'Are you saying they entrapped her father deliberately?'

'Well, it seems likely, doesn't it? The mask is payment for his debts, Colette. Di Mercurio has connections to people who wouldn't think twice about stabbing your father in a back alley, and dumping his body in a canal. Sorry...' he added, as Colette went pale, and Max hissed angrily.

'But what will happen then?' Colette demanded, her voice high with fright. 'He isn't going to give her the mask now, is he? I can't see him ever giving it up. Or maybe it's the other way round. It won't let him.'

'The countess is coming again today. She wants to see what progress he has made,' Rizzo replied, his voice low. 'I don't know what he can say to her. How can he tell her that he won't give her the mask?'

'But what does she want this mask for, anyway?' Max stared at Rizzo. 'She's not going to be able to control it, either.'

The boy shrugged. 'She didn't know that when she asked him to make it, did she? Neither did the master. And what she wants is obvious, cat. Power. The Morezzis are an old family, but not that rich. Her husband is part of the duchess's council, but that doesn't mean all that much, not now that Duchess Olivia has her water magicians to advise her. It's more of an honour than any real responsibility. The countess wants more than that, so they say. She wants the noble houses to have the power and influence they had before, when Duchess Olivia's father was so ill. She wants to carve out her own little kingdom within the city. The mask is supposed to make people do what she wants.'

'It won't, though.' Colette shook her head. 'Why should it do her work for her? It's stronger than that – we've seen it trying to take over both of us. Isn't it just going to make the countess do what *it* wants?' She shivered. 'I bet she'll fight back. Who knows what will happen?'

Rizzo scowled thoughtfully. 'You said it could see what was going on in your head, and it joined in. The mask made you want to pick it up again because you thought it would undo whatever it was you'd done to Max. It's cunning – it's not all about force, is it? It works with what's already there inside you.'

Colette swallowed. 'My father wants to be the most famous maskmaker in the city,' she said, very quietly. 'Perhaps it knew that too. Wherever it came from, whatever's deep down inside it, knew he wouldn't mind bending the rules. Not if it meant his name would be known for ever.'

Rizzo nodded. 'And it'll be the same for the

countess. It'll work with what she gives it. The mask's all about power too. I bet it wouldn't mind helping in the countess's little revolution. Although I wouldn't like to say how long Countess Morezzi would last afterwards.'

'This is madness.' Colette shook her head. 'He's not going to give it to her, surely. What will she do when he says she can't have it?'

'And then what will the mask do, if its maker is threatened?' Max added, and his low mewing growl of a voice made both of them shudder.

Colette was lurking behind the counter, crouching down so that the countess couldn't see her. She might not be an accomplished magician, like her father, but she was sure she was just as strong as Rizzo. If the countess set her servants on the maskmaker, Colette would do her best to protect him. Or if Max was right, and the mask decided to fight back, she supposed she would have to fight to protect the countess too, even if she'd prefer to let her suffer.

Her father had sent the two clerks out for an hour. Even though he looked as if he was sleepwalking, he clearly still had enough control to get the innocents out of the way. He'd sent Colette to her room – but he hadn't said anything about how long she needed to stay there. Not that she would have listened, anyway.

Now he was standing by the window, the silvery mask gripped tightly in his hands. He had threaded ribbons onto the mask now, Colette noticed. He must have done it that very morning. He had used the silver ribbons that she had embroidered with tiny black and white cats, dancing up and down the lengths. It made Colette's skin crawl to see her work adorning that mask. She hoped the cats would pounce, and tangle up all the layers of spells her father had used to build the thing. But she couldn't even feel her embroidery spell now – it was too hidden in the humming hugeness of the silver mask and its magic.

Her father stepped back, pressing the mask against his waistcoat and almost doubling over, as if the strength of it had hit him, hard. He half lifted the mask to his face, but then lowered his hands again with an effort. He was trying not to put it on, she realised, glancing at Rizzo and Max, who were watching as closely as she was. He was resisting. Colette supposed that he wanted to explain to the countess without the mask on, to excuse his behaviour first.

The door swung open, and two tall footmen ushered the countess inside. Perhaps she knew what was coming, Colette thought, seeing their broad shoulders. Was she planning to take the mask by force? Her father's messages pleading for more time, for the project to be cancelled, must have made her suspect something.

'My lady.' The maskmaker bowed low.

'Is this my mask?' the countess demanded, subsiding onto one of the gilded chairs with a puff of skirts, and waving at the mask in his hands. Her footmen took up positions on either side of her, their faces blank.

'It was, my lady,' the maskmaker agreed. 'But I have to tell you – I can no longer sell this mask.'

She stared back at him coldly. 'Why?'

'It will not let me, my lady. The mask has bonded itself to me.' As he spoke, his hands rose up, bringing the mask towards his face in one smooth motion. Colette and Max peered around the edge of the shop counter, fascinated, as the mask lifted out of his hands and floated in the air. In a silvery haze of spells, it sealed itself across his eyes, and the ribbons knotted behind his head – and then disappeared. It seemed that they dissolved into the air.

Colette caught her breath. If the mask no longer needed ribbons to hold it in place, then it must be stuck to his face somehow. Did that mean her father could never take it off?

'It is not mine to sell, my lady,' Colette's father said, his voice deep and hollow. 'The mask belongs to itself, now. And I belong to it.'

'We had an agreement,' the countess hissed. She sprang up, reaching for the silver mask, but then she drew her hand back, nursing it against her dress as if she had been stung. The two footmen started forward, as if they would seize the maskmaker. 'What did you do?'

'Nothing, my lady. The mask does not want to be touched.'

'That's impossible,' she screeched. 'You swore to make the mask for me. It is mine! You know what will happen, Sorani!'

'Nothing will happen. I will fulfil our agreement.'

'What? But you said—' She collapsed back onto her chair, waving back her footmen.

'I will make more masks. They will be finished in a few weeks. One for you, and one for Signor Di Mercurio. The work will go faster now. I will instruct my apprentice.'

Colette glanced towards Rizzo, standing in the doorway, and saw him pale. 'He can't,' she whispered to Max. 'He can't do that – he must know what will happen to Rizzo.'

The cat rubbed his face against her cheek. 'I'm not

sure how much your father is thinking any more.'

'Is he even still there?' Colette whispered. 'Underneath?'

'That is...satisfactory,' the countess admitted. Colette could see her twisting her fingers together, trying to control her eagerness, but she kept her voice icy. 'Two masks will make up for the time you have wasted, I suppose.' She stood up, smoothing down her pink satin skirts, and nodded. 'Very well. I will send my page to you, for news of your work. I trust you will not keep us waiting much longer, Signor Sorani.'

The countess swept out, trying to look dignified but, even as she left, she was still peering eagerly at the mask.

'You can come out, Colette.' The maskmaker turned around, gazing towards the counter. Colette shuddered at the sight of his eyes, night-black inside the holes of the mask. 'I can see you there, hiding.' He chuckled. 'Don't look so horrified, Rizzo. It's no special power of the mask. My daughter is too nosy for her own good, and I could see the edge of her skirt. And that cat kept sticking his head around the side of the counter.'

'Did not,' Max muttered, and then hissed as Colette glared at him. She stood up, folding her arms and staring at her father.

'Don't look so scared, child,' he murmured, crossing the room to stroke her hair.

'Please take it off,' Colette begged.

'Don't you like it?' Something in the timbre of his voice had changed, Colette decided. There was a clanging, metallic note to it now, and it made the hairs rise up on the back of her neck.

'I'd rather see you,' she murmured, trying to lighten her voice. To hide from the mask how much she hated it.

'This *is* me, Colette.' He ran his hand over her hair again, and Colette froze still, so as not to flinch away.

CHAPTER NINE

SIGNOR SORANI SAT DOWN IN one of the velvet chairs they kept in the shop for the customers, and lounged there, tapping his fingers together, smiling to himself. Beneath the silvery gaze of the mask, his smile looked eerie – almost malign.

'Rizzo, go upstairs, my boy, and find the best of those masks we left drying. We've a lot to do.'

Rizzo stared at him, and then padded slowly out of the room. Colette could hear him dragging himself up the stairs.

Colette opened her mouth to protest – and then stopped. There was no point: the mask was putting the words in her father's mouth now. 'I'll help,' she said quickly, chasing after Rizzo.

She found him sitting slumped by the workbench, staring at his hands.

'You aren't going to help him make them, are you?' she demanded.

Rizzo only shrugged, and didn't look up.

'Rizzo!' Colette smacked him on the shoulder. 'Look at me!'

'I have to.'

'You mustn't,' Colette said flatly. 'What if the same thing happens to you? And these two new masks have *got* to go to the countess and Di Mercurio. Who knows what it would do to you, helping make something like that and then having it taken away? It could kill you!'

'Thanks,' Rizzo muttered.

'Well, there's no point pretending,' Colette said gently. 'You can't help make them. Couldn't you run away?'

‘Where to?’ Rizzo shrugged. He was trying to look as though he wasn’t frightened, but Colette could see him picking at his nails – the skin around them was bleeding.

‘Well – your family.’

‘I’m an apprentice, Colette. I’m bonded to your father’s service, for seven years. I can’t run away. The apprentice spell would just bring me straight back again, even if I did.’

‘This is not right,’ Max muttered, stalking backwards and forwards along the workbench. ‘One of those things is dangerous enough…but *three* of them loose, and with Countess Morezzi – we can’t let this happen.’ He stopped sharply, sat down and glared at them both. ‘We must do something.’

Colette and Rizzo nodded hopefully, and the cat huffed, blowing out his whiskers. ‘Both of you are magicians, and you can’t come up with anything?’

‘We tried, remember?’ Colette slumped against the bench, her chin in her hands. ‘I nearly let the mask take me over. We can’t get close enough to steal the mask, or break it. And even if we did creep up on my father while he was sleeping, and the mask didn't wake him, I don't know if we could get it off his face.' She shivered. 'I don't see what we can do. Except…' She ducked her head down.

'What?' Max came to sniff at her, and Rizzo leaned closer.

'Well – the mask still needs someone to wear it. So at the moment, it needs my father. I suppose if he weren't there – I know the mask would just find someone else, eventually, but it might be weakened for a moment. Long enough for us to attack it.'

'You want to kill your father?' Rizzo asked, his mouth dropping open.

'Of course I don't want to! I just said it was the only thing I could think of! I'm not suggesting we actually do it.'

'A cat could take the mask,' Max said thoughtfully. 'The magic wouldn't work on us.'

'Why not?' Rizzo looked sceptical. 'You can't make spells – you couldn't fight back.'

'Look at the shape of my head, idiot boy,' muttered the cat. 'The mask tried to make you and Colette put it on. How could it do that to a cat? It would fall straight off, however tight you tied the ribbons. It may be able to make me do other things, of course. It gave me speech, after all. But I doubt it could do much else. Cats are much more determined than humans.'

'Contrary, you mean.' But Colette ran her hand lovingly over his ears. 'Do you really think you could? It hurt you so much to move the mask away from me before. And – and would you? You can't be sure it won't make you do something awful.'

'There's only one thing cleverer than a cat, dearest Colette,' Max murmured. He bounded along the workbench and jumped down, running for the door. 'Meet me at the end of the alleyway that leads to the Grand Canal, after supper time. Both of you.'

'It's a trick,' Rizzo muttered crossly. 'He won't even turn up. He just wants us to stand out here in the cold. He's probably back at the shop laughing at us.'

'He missed supper,' Colette pointed out. 'Max would never do that just for a joke.'

'Maybe.'

'Just sit down here.' Colette patted the steps. 'He'll come, I promise. Stop whining.' She stared out at the night-black canal. It looked otherworldly in the dark, with lamplight from the great palazzos shimmering on the water, and the strange humps of the covered gondolas moored close by against the bank. Colette was tired and her mind was full of mask magic, and she jumped at every hiss and ripple. *Please hurry*, she thought to Max, as she gazed down at the slow lap of the water below her feet. *Whatever it is you've gone to find, be quick. I've only known my father a couple of months and yet I can't bear to lose him. And Rizzo doesn't mean to be as rude as he is, I think. I don't want him enslaved to a mask, anyway.*

'Colette!'

'He'll be here soon,' Colette hissed back. 'I told you. Be patient!'

'Colette, *look*!'

She looked up, and blinked. There were more lights now. A hundred tiny twinkling lights seemed to have settled on the water, and for a moment she thought they must be floating candles, sent out on the canal by some society hostess with money to burn. Then she saw that the lights came in pairs, and that they had settled on the moored gondolas.

There was a brush of fur across her feet.

'Good girl,' Max murmured approvingly.

'What is it?' Colette whispered back.

'The only thing cleverer than a cat, dear Colette – a great many cats. I called them. They've come to hear what they must do.'

There was a low, uncertain hiss at this, and Max let out a snarl. 'You heard! I told you what this countess is like. Believe me, we do not want her sort having any more power in our city.'

'*Your* city!' Rizzo said scornfully, and Max whirled around. 'Be very glad they can't understand you, stupid boy. It *is* our city. We know every roof top, every alley. We can go anywhere, and we do. While you fools blunder around in the darkness with lamps, a cat has hurried past you on his own business, and you would have never even seen us.'

'So – they understand you, when you're talking?' Colette asked slowly.

'Of course.' Max's whiskers flickered. 'And they know that I can make you understand. They are impressed with me – most of them. Some, of course, think that I should be drowned, for fraternising with you creatures. But the countess is known for her cruelty, Colette. Not like Duchess Olivia. What did the Little Duchess give her most trusted advisor, after all?'

Colette gazed down at him, uncertainly, and Max's tail twitched.

'He means the cat that Duchess Olivia gave her maid, Etta,' Rizzo told her. 'She made him, remember? Out of a spilled cup of hot chocolate. And then she turned him from a kitten to a full-grown cat, when her cousin left him for dead.'

‘Exactly.’ Max was purring so loudly that Colette could feel the vibration through the leather soles of her slippers; the other cats were purring, too. Several of them leaped down from the gondolas and surged forward, like a tide of striped and spotted fur rising around their feet. Max stood protectively in front of Colette, staring down the other cats. ‘Coco. We’ve all seen him, walking with the duchess, and Mistress Etta. He is part of the duchess’s inner circle of advisors. And the countess is working against them.’

‘We don’t know that for certain,’ Colette said doubtfully. ‘We don’t have any proof that she’s a traitor.’

Max’s eyes glittered, and he hissed. ‘Don’t confuse them, Colette. Not if you want them to help.’

‘She is working against the duchess,’ Rizzo put in. ‘Of course she is. That’s why she wants the mask.’

‘Perhaps we should tell the duchess then,’ Colette suggested.

‘No proof.’ Rizzo shrugged. ‘They’d laugh in our faces, Colette. And then throw us in jail. Count

Morezzi may not be one of the duchess's closest confidantes, but he's still a member of the council. He does have some influence. We can't just accuse his wife of plotting to overthrow the duchess!'

'I suppose not...' Colette sighed. 'So what are we going to do? It needs to be fast, before my father starts making Rizzo work on the new masks.'

'My brothers and sisters will help,' Max told her. 'There are many of us who live in magicians' households. We will try to find spells to counteract the mask, and help us rescue your father from it. But that won't free him from his debt to the countess – or get rid of her greed for power.' He stopped, his whiskers bristling. 'Who's there?'

A thin white cat appeared out of the shadows, and Max sniffed at her, and appeared to listen. Then he turned to Colette, his tail flicking from side to side. 'A page has just come from the countess's house with a message for your father.'

'What message?' Colette demanded worriedly, but Max flattened his ears.

'Go back and find out, Colette! It was handed to your father, that's all the watcher knows.'

'They have cats watching the shop?' Rizzo whispered to Colette.

'We have cats everywhere,' Max pointed out. 'They're just paying more attention to the maskmaker's than usual.'

Colette nodded, and turned to hurry back along the alleyway. Rizzo was following her, but there was a pattering scurry of paws in the darkness too. Were all the cats coming? She couldn't see them in the dimness of the alley, but as they came out into the well-lit square, a hundred shadowy shapes disappeared into corners and dark patches, taking up their positions before the shop.

Colette and Rizzo slipped in through the side door, and then stopped at the foot of the stairs, gazing up. Her father was descending the staircase dressed in a gorgeous dull-silver satin coat and breeches. He had a black tricorne hat pulled low over his masked face, and a dark scarf draped under it, so that not even his mouth and chin could be seen. Colette only recognised him by the tang of magic that she had come to know as his.

'Are – are you going out?' she asked.

'I am going to the Ridotto, to meet the countess.' He sighed. 'She sent a page to summon me, and after this morning, I can't afford to refuse.' His words were regretful, but Colette could hear the edge of excitement in his voice. He was smiling under that dark veil, she was almost sure. 'Perhaps the mask will bring me luck.' He glanced at Rizzo. 'I shall not be back late – be ready to work when I return, boy. We must start the making of the new masks.'

'Sir,' Rizzo whispered reluctantly, as the maskmaker sauntered out through the shop, the silver satin glimmering in the lamplight.

'You can't!' Colette hissed, as the door swung shut. 'You'll have to go, before he comes back.'

'I told you, I don't have anywhere to go! My family would only send me back, or they could be had up by the courts. I'm bound, Colette!' Rizzo twisted his fingers together. 'Perhaps it will be all right. If I'm careful.'

'Careful!' Colette rolled her eyes. 'What difference will being careful make? I suppose you think you can resist the magic better than my father.'

'No.' Rizzo sank down on the bottom step of the staircase with his face in his hands. 'No, I don't. I'm sure those spells work by putting part of your self into the mask – I think that's what your father's done. If we make two more, they'll take even more of him, and part of me too. The countess and Di Mercurio will be wearing half my soul, and what will I be left with?'

'If you can't run away, we'll have to stop them, somehow,' Colette muttered. 'Before you and my father go too far into the making.' Then she frowned down at Rizzo. 'I don't understand. My father said the countess told him to go to the Ridotto. Why? What does she want him there for? Surely he should be hard at work on her new masks, not gambling and dancing and showing off his fine satin coat.'

'There's something else going on here,' Max agreed, sitting down on the step next to Rizzo, and curling his tail tidily around his paws.

'Knowing the master, he'll lose again,' Rizzo suggested, looking into the cat's masked eyes. 'He'll get himself even more into debt to one of the countess's gang of rabble-rousers.'

'Mmmm. Perhaps. But he's already agreed to make the masks. There must be more to it than that.'

'If everyone goes to the Ridotto masked,' Colette murmured, thinking out loud, 'then no one knows who anyone else is. Or they're not supposed to.'

Max purred approvingly. 'Indeed. A very good place for plotting, don't you think? They're not waiting for your father to make the masks. They want him deeper into the conspiracy now.'

'But he likes the Little Duchess,' Rizzo objected. 'He wouldn't plot with them against her. We've made masks for her before. She doesn't wear them often – only for the occasional ceremony where she has to, like the elections. But he was delighted. He said her magic ran through the whole city, and she'd changed it for the better.'

'He must have suspected that the countess wanted the mask for some sort of plot against the throne, though,' Colette pointed out sadly. 'And he still agreed to make it.'

'He didn't have a choice – there's a difference between making her a mask, and actually joining a conspiracy,' Rizzo argued.

'Then why do they want him there?' Colette paused, then looked Rizzo up and down. 'Do you have another coat?'

'What?'

'Is that your only coat, or do you have another one?'

'My old one, but it's too short in the arms…' Rizzo said slowly. 'What does it matter whether I have more than one coat?'

'Fetch it.' Colette pushed past him up the stairs. 'And breeches, if you have those. Meet me in the workroom.'

‘What are you doing?’ Max demanded, as he sprang up the steps beside her.

‘We need to find out what the countess is planning, and how my father is caught up in it. And we can’t go to the Ridotto like this, can we?’ Colette waved at her dress, which was one of the cambric ones her father had ordered for her – pretty, but nowhere near grand enough for a great gathering of nobles. ‘We need to fit in, and I haven’t time to make us clothes the proper way.’ She darted into her room, and snatched her oldest skirt and bodice from the clothes chest. Then, almost as an afterthought, she took the pieces of blue watered silk that she had brought with her from her old home.

Rizzo followed her into the workroom, and laid out a threadbare coat and breeches on the workbench. ‘I could get a couple of *soldi* for this coat, you know, if I took it to one of the market stalls. What are you going to do with it? Am I getting it back?’

‘Yes.’ Colette sighed. ‘You will. And it’ll be worth a lot more. Be quiet, can’t you? I’m thinking.’ Then she snatched his hand. 'I need to borrow magic from you – I haven't enough, not to do this quickly.'

Rizzo yelped as she grabbed his wrist and pressed both their hands against his old coat. 'Ow! What are you…' But his voice died away to a whisper as the fabric began to change. The rough, faded woollen cloth softened and darkened to a smooth dark green satin. He gasped as Colette bit hard into the ball of her thumb and shook a tiny drop of blood out onto the coat, where it spread and flowered into scarlet embroidery around the skirts, and up the front and in and out of the buttonholes. 'That's not a spell the master taught you!' he hissed. Colette ignored him as she brushed a tear from her eyes – biting her thumb had hurt – and crystal buttons stitched themselves down the front. 'Where did you get the power to do this?'

'I got it from both of us. Ssshhh, I'm thinking. There.' She picked up the coat, and the matching breeches, and swirled it admiringly, smiling as the crystal buttons glittered in the candlelight. 'Go and change. Don't forget you'll need a mask too. Better make it one of the plainer ones, or my father will recognise it.'

She heard the door click behind her as she turned to her own faded dress – one that she had loved when Ma made it for her, but sadly worn by now. The thin grey cotton was rubbing into holes in the creases, and the faint pink stripe was hardly there. 'The same but grander,' Colette murmured to herself. 'What would you have made me, Ma, if I could have had anything? If I was yours, but not? A girl who goes to parties in silks and satins…' She stroked the soft cotton, remembering. There had been one dress – a cream-coloured silk, with pale pink stripes, made for the young daughter of a spice merchant. Ma had held the fabric up against Colette, smiling and then sighing.

'It's only for pretend,' Colette promised the memory of her mother. 'I'm not turning into one of those spoiled little rich girls.' She had refused a grand silk dress when her father suggested it. 'Just this once,' she murmured. 'I don't even know how long it will stay. Perhaps in the morning it'll just be cotton again.' She spread her fingers across the fabric and closed her eyes, daydreaming the dress. The pink stripes would shimmer and glow, like the pink dawn light in the sky that morning. Only that morning! Colette shook her head to dislodge a sudden wave of weariness. So much had happened since she had woken up to the dawn sky spreading across her coverlet.

The fabric in her hands grew heavier, and she heard the stiff rustle of silk. Colette opened her eyes, looking down at the dress. She was clutching the best ivory silk, gleaming in the candlelight, and striped with the glimmering pink of dawn clouds. There was a stomacher too, made from the blue silk, as if the pale morning sky had brightened to glorious midday. The blue was embroidered with tiny butterflies, so delicately stitched they made her sigh with pleasure. She ran her fingers over the raised goldwork of their bodies, wondering if they were really there, or if all her spell had created was the illusion of a dress.

'Put it on, then,' Max mewed. 'Hurry. Your father

is already at the Ridotto, remember. There isn't much time.'

Colette eyed the bodice, chewing her lip. She hadn't remembered that she would need to actually get into the dress. It was made in the height of fashion, she could tell. The skirt was draped over panniers almost as wide as the countess's. It needed at least one maid, possibly two, and all she had was Rizzo, and a cat.

She unlaced her old bodice, and stepped out of her skirt, standing there in her shift. Should she call Maria and Lina, and try to explain? But how? They would never let her go. Someone patted her shoulder, and Colette jumped, thinking that it was Rizzo, back from changing. And he had seen her in her underdress!

A faint, sweet scent of lavender eddied around her, just a hint of the smell, like clothes packed away in a chest with a sachet of dried herbs, the way Ma had liked to store them. Work-callused hands stroked over Colette's, and she closed her eyes, shivering. Someone was lacing up the dress, pinning in the bodice and settling the horsehair panniers around her waist. Someone fluffed out the lace at her elbows – her old shift had lace on it now, without her noticing. Someone twitched the skirts so they fell just to the ground, leaving rose-pink satin slippers showing. Colette stood still, waiting, and the lavender scent swirled, then faded.

Colette opened her eyes. She looked at Max – but he was staring determinedly out of the crack between the shutters, the fur along his backbone stiffly raised. 'Did you see?' she whispered, but he only swished his tail, and leaned further towards the window.

The door opened, and she turned to Rizzo, smiling as she saw him in the green coat and breeches. His shirt was snowy linen, now, and he too had falls of lace at his neck and cuffs.

He stared at her. 'I never thought you could look like that,' he murmured. And then, embarrassed, he went to the masks hanging on the wall, and lifted down a beaked *bauta* mask, and the tricorne hat to go with it, and wrapped the mantle around his shoulders.

With his face covered, he looked quite different, suddenly taller and older. Colette took a step back, surprised.

He looked around the walls for a mask for Colette, and reached for a pale pink confection, studded with butterflies, their wings trembling as his fingers came near.

'No,' Colette whispered. 'That one.' She pointed to a small golden mask, half hidden behind another on the wall. It was a little faded and dusty, but still beautiful. Colette hated the thought of wearing a mask at all – she didn't want to look like a stranger, the way that mask had made her mother look, so many years before. But she had to, and at least in the little gold mask she could imagine her mother was there to help her again.

They stared at each other shyly, two strangers, until Max leaped down from the workbench and brushed himself around Colette's skirts.

'Time to go.'

Chapter Ten

COLETTE PEERED THROUGH THE DOORWAY at the press of people. She had never seen a place like this, not from the inside. Huge glass chandeliers hung from the coffered wooden ceiling on gilded chains, and the crowds chattered and danced and flirted in their flickering light.

The bright dresses and black tricornes and mantles stood out against the dark red walls in a blaze of colour, but it was the noise that Colette found so confusing. It seemed to batter against her ears, rolling back and forth like the waves on the sea.

'Go on, then,' Rizzo hissed in her ear. 'Don't just stand there. You've got a mask on, remember. No one knows it's you.'

Colette stepped unwillingly into the room, her hand lightly placed on Rizzo's arm. They were posing as a couple, which made it seem all the more odd. 'Can you see my father?' she whispered. 'Or the countess? I'd recognise at least one of her dresses. She has a blue silk, like my bodice…'

They strolled together around the suite of rooms, smiling and bowing occasionally. 'People are staring,' Colette whispered in Rizzo's ear.

'Well, your dress is very…nice,' he muttered. 'You look quite grand. Perhaps they're wondering who you are.'

'Maybe I should have made us plainer things,' Colette worried. 'I didn't think we'd be so conspicuous.'

'It's all right. We've got the masks on.' He turned to look at her, and she thought he was smiling under his. 'Aren't you excited?'

'No!' Colette hissed. 'Are you mad? It must be because you've got a mask on – they just send people silly. They're dangerous – they should be banned.'

'And then your father and I would lose our livelihood, and you wouldn't have a home,' Rizzo pointed out. 'Come on. We need to keep looking.' He pulled her after him into the next room, which was full of card tables. Here the noise was much less. Heads were down over the tables, and the players spoke in low voices. Even those standing watching were still, absorbed by the movement of the cards – and the piles of money.

'Look,' Colette whispered, patting Rizzo's arm. 'Over there, another doorway. I'm sure I just saw a flash of blue silk under that woman's cloak. I'd know that fabric anywhere. I think it's her.'

They strolled through the room slowly, so as not to look too obviously as if they were following, but at the door their way was suddenly barred by a tall man in a dark red livery, without a mask. 'This is a private room, signorina,' he said flatly. 'Invitation only.'

Rizzo tugged Colette away before she could argue. 'What did you do that for?' she muttered, stalking back across the card room. 'That was one of the countess's footmen. I recognised him. They're in there! We could have said we were invited.'

'As if that would work! If they're bothering to keep people out, they're going to check, aren't they?' Rizzo peered at her, his eyes dark and eerie in the holes of the white mask. 'This is good, Colette, don't you see? It's definitely them, and they are plotting something if they're tucked away in a private room. Now we just have to get ourselves in there.' He drew her back into a shadowy corner of the card room. 'How, though?'

'The door is open,' Colette said thoughtfully, peering at it. 'There's a screen beyond it so one can't see who's inside, but we could slip through the gap. The footman only stopped us because he didn't recognise us. If we could just get in without him seeing.'

'Yes, *just*...'

'Don't be rude.' Colette smiled at Rizzo, and pulled

him into a corner, behind a tall candelabra. With the glittering candlelight in front of them, they were almost completely hidden. 'Can you spin?'

'What?'

'Can you spin wool? Oh, never mind. Here. They should dust better.' She reached up to the angle of the two walls and tugged down a fine hank of spiders' webs. Rizzo hissed in disgust as she draped a web across the front of his silk coat. 'Keep still – this is difficult,' Colette murmured, stretching one hand up into the air. 'And do try not to make a noise. We don't want anyone to notice us.'

'But spiders…' he muttered. 'I don't like them. Oh!'

Colette had brought her hand down again, and with it a strand of fine greyish thread, not unlike the spider silk, but softer.

'What is it?'

'Shadows…ssshhh…' She went on spinning, drawing the shadows out into thread, and weaving them with the spiders' webs into a fine grey cloak.

She draped the shimmering fabric around their shoulders and drew it over their heads in a deep hood. 'No one will see us now,' she whispered at last. 'Pull it tight, around your face.'

'Won't it break? It's only spiders' webs…'

Colette breathed out a laugh. 'No. Think how strong shadows are. They're always there, just beyond the light, aren't they? That's all we have to worry about – if someone holds a light right up to us, then they might see through.' She caught his hand. 'Come on. We'd better go now, before I lose my nerve.'

Together they padded back through the card room to the screened door, and the tall footman, listening to the whisper and rustle of Colette's silk frock and the faint hiss of the shadow cloak on the polished wooden boards.

The footman stared past them, looking bored, and they slipped by, Colette twitching the hem of the cloak away from his shining black shoes.

Once they had rounded the tall painted screen, the inner room was revealed as far more luxurious than the card room and the other apartments of the Ridotto. Its wooden ceiling had been plastered over and painted in garlands of white and blue, with dancing nymphs in each corner. A rich plaster wreath stood in the very centre, with a chandelier hanging from it, filled with tall wax candles. Colette and Rizzo drew back against the side wall, away from its revealing glow.

Below the chandelier stood a table, scattered with playing cards and scraps of paper scrawled with promises to pay. Colette's father sat there, huddled in his mantle, a pitifully small pile of coins by his hand. But it seemed the game had been forgotten. The cards had been cast aside, and the players were leaning close across the table, talking.

'I cannot, my lady,' the maskmaker said, as Colette and Rizzo drew further back into the shadow of the heavy blue satin curtains. Colette cursed the size of the stupid, fashionable panniers in her skirt – but she could feel the shadows softening and melting together with those she had woven into her cloak, and her pulse slowed. They were well hidden.

'You must. You will be well rewarded. Not just by the forgiveness of your debts – your *many* debts.' The countess smiled down at the pile of papers in front of her. 'There will be a new ruling class, Sorani. Why shouldn't you be part of it?'

'I consented to make you a mask, that was all. That was my first mistake.'

Colette could hear the bitterness in her father's voice. He sounded real again, more like himself, and she glanced hopefully around at Rizzo. Perhaps he wasn't completely under the spell of the mask – yet.

'But making a mask to enhance your own powers of persuasion was one thing, my lady. It would only have worked if you had the hearts of your listeners already, if they were open to your voice. Outright rebellion is another matter entirely. I will not join.' He twitched then, and pressed his hand against the silver forehead of the mask.

'I don't think your mask agrees with you, Sorani,' said a tall man on the other side of the table, with a laugh. His mask was a grand sunburst, gold and gleaming, and there was a warmth to him that reminded Colette of sunlight. He was beautiful, but dangerous. Strong enough to burn her up. She wriggled a little further back into the shadow of the curtains.

'I think the mask loves the thought of our little rebellion next week. It wants to call to all those poor, hungry, downtrodden people, and promise them something better than a self-obsessed girl as their ruler.'

Deep in the shadows Colette clenched her fingers tight – how could the countess delude herself so? *She* was the one who wanted power, not Olivia, who had been born to it, and never given a choice.

'You'll have your own masks, soon enough,' Colette's father snapped. 'I have promised.'

'But the Wedding of the Sea is next week. I need the masks by then, we have – plans.' The countess banged her hand down on the table. 'I can't wait another year. I won't! Not another year of that simpering girl on the throne, another year of standing in the background. The whole of the city will be there and watching. We must start then!'

'I...will...not.' The words came out in a pained growl, as if Colette's father had to force them through the lips of the mask.

Colette felt Rizzo squeeze her hand, and she looked up at him, her eyes wide with relief. Her father was not a traitor – not yet. 'Perhaps we can find some way of proving what she's doing,' she whispered. 'We could denounce her. We could post evidence in one of the lions' mouths, the secret postboxes.' She had passed them so many times in the streets, but the yawning stone mouths still made her shudder. One of Alyssa's cousins had been accused – over some shady business deal that had gone wrong, Alyssa claimed. The man he'd cheated had posted a message denouncing him, and the council's men had stolen him out of his very bed and thrown him into the Pozzi, the damp cells by the duke's palace. 'They're anonymous – no one would know it was us.'

'The chambers under the lions' heads get opened by the council, Colette. Count Morezzi isn't going to let anyone denounce his wife, is he?'

'I suppose… Then perhaps we should all just leave? We could persuade my father, I'm sure. We could go and live somewhere else, far away from Venice.'

'And leave *them* to plot against the duchess?' Rizzo muttered. 'No.'

'Then what can we do?' Colette demanded angrily. 'They won't let him live, will they, if he's not part of their conspiracy? They'll get rid of him! We can't let that happen.' In her desperation, she raised her voice, and even went to stamp her foot. The curtains billowed outwards, just a little.

'Ssshhh!' Rizzo clapped his hand across her mouth, but it was too late. Di Mercurio sprang up, snatching up a candelabra from the table and stalking to their hiding place so quickly that Colette was sure he must be using magic. She hadn't realised he was a magician. She pressed back against Rizzo, her fingers flickering as she tried to strengthen the weaving of the cloak. But she was scared. She could feel the shadow-threads thinning and shredding as the candlelight shone down.

He could see her.

But not Rizzo. Hurriedly, she thrust the bundle of shadows behind her, covering Rizzo with another layer. Then she stepped out from behind the curtain, shaking out her pink-striped skirts and glaring at Di Mercurio.

The countess and Colette's father stared at her in confusion, and then at last her father recognised her under the mask. He started up from the table in horror. 'Colette! What are you doing here?'

'This is his daughter?' the countess snapped. 'Daniel, seize her, at once!' She laughed. 'Yes, now I recognise you, child. I didn't see you for what you were, in those fine feathers. The dressmaker's brat.'

'Don't speak to her that way,' Colette's father snarled. 'Colette, go home, now. Hurry! They have a spell for quiet across that door, no one will hear you if you scream! What did you think you were doing?'

'I imagine she came to spy on you.' The countess snorted. 'The poor little dear thought she would help. Daniel, for pity's sake, hold onto her! Don't you realise what we have here? Now our friend will do anything we like!'

Signor Di Mercurio seized Colette's wrist and pulled her against him, wrapping an arm around her tightly. 'She has power,' he warned. 'I can feel it.'

'Well, so do you! She's a child, Daniel, don't be so feeble.'

Colette jerked her head at Rizzo, still hidden in the cloak of shadows. She could see him only because the spell was hers, and he was a faint creature, no more than a shadowy form in the darkness. If she hadn't known he was there, she would almost have said he was a trick of the light. He stood hesitating, the shadow-form shaking slightly – and then he made for the door, a faint shimmering in the air the only sign of his passing.

Colette took a deeper breath, and stamped on Di Mercurio's foot to make sure he was distracted.

‘Ah! Little brat!’ He twisted her arm up behind her back, making her catch her breath with pain.

‘Don’t do that to her!’ Colette’s father overturned his chair as he made for Di Mercurio.

‘Stand back, maskmaker!’ The countess laughed, and stepped delicately to stand between them. ‘Children are so fragile. So easily harmed. I really wouldn’t get any closer.’ She patted his cheek in a horrible gesture of affection. ‘Now. Are you going to do what we want?’

‘Yes,’ Colette’s father groaned. ‘Yes, I’ll do it. Whatever you want. Let her go. Colette, come here to me. Ugh…’ He groaned suddenly, clutching at his face, and almost doubling over with pain.

‘What is it?’ Colette cried, struggling in Di Mercurio’s arms.

The countess stepped forward, fascinated. ‘It’s the mask. How very interesting… His resistance to its magic is weakening. Its power is strengthened as he becomes less himself.’ She chuckled to herself. ‘I wonder how much longer our dear maskmaker will last. So lucky that we only need him for a few more days…' Then she frowned. 'Remind me, Daniel, that we must secure the apprentice. He will know how to make more masks for us – and how to make sure that these new masks are a little more biddable.'

'No!' Colette shrieked, twisting and pulling against her captor. 'Let me go! I have to help my father. And Rizzo will never make masks for you, never, never!'

She squirmed sideways, trying to get close enough to Di Mercurio's wrist to bite, but he only held her tighter, so tight she could barely breathe. Colette went limp, and suddenly remembered her magic. Why was she struggling so stupidly, when she could use her spells instead?

A sudden cloud of yellow butterflies filled the air, fluttering up from her embroidered stomacher. They swirled in Di Mercurio's face, blinding him with their dusty wings, and pressing against his mouth and nose.

'Faugh!' He let go of her at once, frantically brushing at his face, beating at the tiny creatures in horror. They swirled and fluttered and danced, easily avoiding his hands, and darting in to settle on him again.

'Idiot!' The countess grabbed Colette by the shoulders, and slapped her. 'Don't you dare try anything like that with me, you little horror. I am not afraid of butterflies.' Her fingers were iron-hard through the silk of Colette's dress, and she shook her to and fro, so that Colette's teeth chattered and rattled in her head.

'Let go of me!'

'Is that likely? I need you, little one. You are going to make sure that your father does exactly as I say. Just a few more days, that's all.'

'And then what?' Colette snarled, glancing towards the door. Where had Rizzo gone? She wondered if he was coming back. But what could he do? There was only him – and a gang of cats. How could they rescue her?

Di Mercurio was still tearing at his face, spitting with disgust, but he had wafted away most of the butterflies by now, they were swooping and diving around the chandelier instead. Soon, he would be able to seize her again, and this time he would be sure not to let her go. He would spell her into submission. She had to get herself free now. Desperate, Colette shut her eyes and spoke to the blue silk dress the countess wore – the dress she and Ma had worked on for so long, made from the same silk as the stomacher for her own dress. Their last dress. *Help me, Ma*, she thought pleadingly, pressing her fingers against the blue silk over her ribs. *You helped before. You never wanted anything to do with magic, but please help me now.*

Would they remember her, her little golden fish? She flexed her fingers against the countess's sleeve, calling to the golden threads stitched in and out of the water-blue silk. She spoke to them gently, sending the tiny fish gliding through the silken water towards the countess. They changed as they swam, growing stronger and thicker and heavier, and the countess let out a scream as golden chains appeared suddenly around her wrists, binding her hands behind her back.

Colette stumbled away, rubbing her shoulders, and the chains swam on, cutting through the air as if it were water, and seizing upon Di Mercurio. Colette smiled faintly, remembering the hours and hours of embroidering those fish. She should have been glad that there were so many…

Di Mercurio was chanting, a low, furious whisper. Colette wasn't sure how long the chains would hold – they looked solid but, deep down, they knew they were only golden threads. She collapsed on her knees beside her father, snatching his hands in hers. The mask was glowing, and it was hard to see where her father's face ended and the mask began. The dark mantle had torn aside, and half his head seemed to be encased in gleaming silver.

'Papa!'

She caught her breath. It was the first time she had called him that. It was the first time she had called him anything but 'sir' – she hadn't known what to say, so she had said nothing. 'Papa…' She stumbled over it, but he heard her – perhaps because of the name she had called him. His hands tightened on her own, and the mask's light dimmed.

'Colette! Run! Before Di Mercurio gets them free. The mask will force me to help them, I can feel it. I can't fight against it any longer. If you're still here, I can't protect you.'

'But I can't just leave you,' Colette whispered. 'Can't you come with us? There's only a footman outside the door. Come now – run! We'll run away from the city.'

Her father's whole body twitched and spasmed, and his hand suddenly clenched on hers, squeezing it so that the bones of her fingers grated, and Colette screamed in pain.

'NO!' the maskmaker roared, and he tore himself away, writhing on the floor and wrenching at the mask, scraping and ripping at his own face.

Colette huddled by the table leg, weeping at the pain in her hand and the sight of her father. He was changing and disappearing before her eyes. The silvery satin of his coat and breeches was starting to glow in the same way as the mask. Soon, there would be nothing of him left.

It was then, just when Colette had lost all hope, that the window shattered, and a tide of parti-coloured fur leaped in, spangled with diamond shards of glass. Colette stared at the window, gasping, and then laughing with mixed relief and fright, her good hand pressed against her mouth to hold back the noise. After the cats came Rizzo, standing pale-faced in the opening, still cloaked in shreds of shadow.

'Are you all right?' he gasped. 'We heard you scream – that was when Max sprang. We were climbing along the balconies and ledges, trying to find a window open, but then he just threw himself at the glass. There's magic in him, Colette, there must be, I've never seen a cat leap so high.' He glanced frantically around the room, his eyes widening as he saw the countess and Di Mercurio fighting against their golden chains, and Colette's father tearing at his face.

'The mask...' Colette gasped out. 'My father – it's almost taken him, I don't know how to stop it.'

'They do.' Rizzo jumped down, crouching beside Colette and hauling her up. 'Look.'

Like some great fur coat, the cats had covered her father. Each of them might only be small, but there were at least a hundred cats pinning him to the floor, stretching him out for Max. The unearthly glow seeped through their fur, so their eyes shone eerily, and each hair of their coats was outlined in silvery light.

Max stood on her father's chest, hissing furiously in his face – his whiskers touching the mask.

'Colette. You must tell me. Should I do this? I don't know what will happen – I don't know how much of your father is left underneath.'

'Yes,' Colette sobbed. 'He hates it, I know he does. Wait, and I'll help you.'

'No.'

Max shot out one thin dappled paw, and scratched a great furrow down the silvery forehead, across the nose and mouth – and then again, and again.

Colette turned aside, burying her face in the shadows trailing from Rizzo's shoulders.

'Colette, it's all right. It's working,' Rizzo whispered. 'Max must have some of its magic inside him. He's tearing it apart.'

'But my father,' Colette whispered. 'Is he even there?' The shrieking, ripping noise of claws tearing through layer upon layer of spells had ceased – now there was only a strange silence and, beyond it, the hum and chatter of the crowds partying in the assembly rooms.

'I am.'

Colette lifted her head slowly, forcing herself to look.

Her father was standing there, with Max in his arms. The cat looked weary, his whiskers drooping, a dull grey dust coating his fur. But he was purring, a low, triumphant note that made Colette's heart beat faster. She held out her arms, and he leaped into them, nestling against her shoulder and dabbing his cold nose in the hollow of her neck.

'You saved me.' Her father's voice was low, and each word was half a cough. His hair was white with the same dust that covered Max. Except that as Colette came closer, she saw that it wasn't. It was just white. Silvery-white, like a man thirty years older. And his face was lined and creased with pain.

'No, it was Max. You're still…you?' she whispered.

'I think so. The mask is gone – I can't feel its magic controlling me any longer. Although I'm not sure how much magic is left in me at all,' he admitted. 'Rizzo, you may have more power than your master.'

'It will come back,' Rizzo said staunchly. 'When you're back in your workroom, sir. What do we do with them?' He nodded at the countess and Di Mercurio, still in their chains, and now guarded by rows and rows of silent, staring cats. Di Mercurio was no longer whispering angry spells – the thin gold chains had spread, coiling up his arms and chest, and over his mouth. The countess was backing slowly away from the cats, pressing herself up against the wall as they advanced.

Colette's father shuddered. 'Send a message to the palace. The duchess is known as a lover of cats. She will be most interested, when she hears of this. I expect she knows enough of Di Mercurio to suspect what has been happening, even if she isn't aware of the countess's part in the conspiracy.'

At his words, the same white cat who had brought the message earlier in the evening broke out of the ring of guards, and padded over to the window, neatly avoiding the broken glass. She disappeared out into the night.

'Do you think we can go?' Colette murmured in Max's ear. 'I don't want to stay here and have to explain…' She looked down at her cat, surprised that he didn't answer. But he was staring at her with great yellow eyes.

'Oh! You can't! Max, you used your scrap of magic. Your talking's gone.' She gazed back at him sadly, but he butted his head against her chin, hard enough to make her laugh. 'I suppose you never much liked it anyway. And I do still know what you mean. I think.' She hitched him closer against her shoulder, and stretched out her hand to her father. 'Let's go home.'

'I still think you should be in bed. You could have died, last night!' Colette glared disapprovingly at her father.

'I'm not leaving you and Rizzo alone in my workroom,' her father murmured, lifting his head from the cushions. Rizzo and the shop clerks had carried one of the gilt sofas from the shop upstairs, so that he could recover in comfort. Colette's sewing table was next to him, crammed with cordials, and scented salts, and Maria's lucky rabbit's foot, which she swore had cured her grandfather's palsy.

Colette folded her lips tightly. She thought that was hardly fair – after all, it was her father who had created a mask that had half swallowed his soul. From the expression on Rizzo's face, he was thinking the same thing.

Her father sputtered a weak laugh. 'I can see you scowling, Rizzo. I know what you're thinking. But at least my spells don't blow up... Start a mask, then, boy. Show me something beautiful to help me mend.'

Rizzo nodded eagerly, and picked up a papier-mâché base, running his fingers over the smooth white features, feeling the tiny imperfections in the paper skin. 'Perhaps a harlequin?' he murmured, and a snatch of diamond patterning shimmered in the air above the mask. Then the spell disappeared with sharp pop as he stared out of the window.

'Tch...' Colette's father muttered. 'Control, Rizzo, control...'

'There's a cat outside the window, sir!' Rizzo hissed back.

Max, who had been stretched along the cushioned arm of the sofa, leaped up, the fur along his back rising. Then he seemed to recognise the white cat at the window, springing to the sill and nudging

Rizzo's arm to encourage him to undo the catch.

The white cat leaned in and nuzzled at Max, rubbing the side of her face against his. Then she jumped gracefully down inside the workroom, and gazed around at Rizzo, Colette and her father, then back up to the window, almost as if she was making an introduction.

A huge chocolate-coloured cat sprang onto the sill, and stared gravely in at them. His coat gleamed with a sheen of magic, and he wore a silver collar, flashing with jewels. Tucked into it was a piece of folded paper.

'Coco!' Colette breathed. Mistress Etta's cat. The one that Duchess Olivia had made for her from spilled chocolate. She glanced anxiously at Max, hoping he wouldn't object to this stranger on his windowsill. But Max had flattened his ears submissively and simply stared at the visitor.

The chocolate cat lowered his head, obviously encouraging Rizzo to take the note from under his collar.

Rizzo reached out cautiously. 'It's addressed to you, Colette.' He handed her the folded message, and Colette opened it, scanning the pretty, pointed script. Her hands shook as she read it out loud.

My dearest Signorina Colette,

Our great thanks to you for the message that arrived at the palace last night. My mages found Countess Morezzi and Signor di Mercurio at the Ridotto as you described, wrapped in remarkably fine golden chains. Both of them have decided that they feel quite weary of city life, and they have decided to retire to their country estates on the mainland.

I regret deeply that I never made the acquaintance of your mother, Madame Harriet, who taught you to create such exquisite dresses. Should you wish to reopen your mother's shop when you come of age, or to purchase an establishment of your own, a sum of money has been deposited in your name with the Guldoni Bank. I hope that you will allow me, and my cousin Lady Mia, to be your first clients.

Please pass on my admiration to your father, Signor Sorani, and his apprentice, the boy Rizzo. Their skill is unsurpassed – thankfully, perhaps. An amount of gold has been banked for the boy also, as my informants tell me that he played a vital role in the action.

With my warmest wishes and gratitude,

Olivia Venetia

THE END

Turn the page for a sneak peek at the next Magical Venice book:

THE GIRL OF GLASS

The old man got up, and began searching the shelves, humming happily to himself as he gathered ingredients from the jars and bottles into a small stone bowl. Mariana watched him curiously, her nose twitching as she caught the scents of the spices and powders he was stirring together. This magic was so different from her father's. The glassmaker breathed his magic into his creations, joining the spell and the molten glass together in the darkness of the workshop. It was an ancient tradition, and deeply valued in the city – her father was an important man. His apprentices were boys chosen for the spark of magic deep inside them. Rafa and Giorgio would spend years working with her father, mostly doing the boring, menial tasks, in the hope that their magic would one day develop the same way his had, and they would be great glassmaker-magicians themselves. There were no spells, though, not like this. Mariana's fingers shifted, and she realised that she was twisting her hands together in excitement.

'You can come and watch.' Signor Nesso glanced up at her. 'You're not afraid of magic, then.'

'My father is a glassmaker-magician,' Mariana explained, hopping up and leaning over the bench to peer into the bowl. 'This looks like – like a recipe. Like our cook pounding herbs. It's so different.'

'A glassmaker. Lucky child, to be so surrounded with beautiful things.'

Mariana sniffed. 'Beautiful things that sing with magic for other people. All I'm allowed to do is dust them. Is this a spell? Do you have words for it? Or does it just happen by itself, the way my father's magic does?'

'There are words, but they don't matter so much,' the old man explained, smiling down at her. Mariana wondered if he was lonely. He seemed to be enjoying the chance to show off the spell. As though he wanted someone to talk to. She glanced around the shop, suddenly realising how empty it was. She had expected a shop on the Piazza to be far busier than this.

'People don't linger in magic shops. Not usually. They sneak in, and hurry out.'

Mariana blinked, and then thought very hard about

fish, to see what would happen. She didn't like the old man sifting through her thoughts.

'Yes, very nice.' He lifted his hand from the marble pestle that he'd been using to grind the ingredients together, and twisted it swiftly in the air in front of Mariana. A tiny, silvery fish appeared gasping on his palm, and Mariana squeaked.

'Well, you'd better catch the poor little thing. Put it in a jar. There's a jug of water on the end of the bench.'

'You made him!' Mariana snatched the little fish, and dropped it into an empty glass jar, watching guiltily as it writhed about, desperate for water. She almost knocked over the jug, as she raced to fill the jar, but then she felt it lifted out of her hands, pouring a stream of water over the tiny fish. The silvery creature righted itself immediately, gliding through the glittering cascade with dreamy sweeps of its long fins.

'From your thoughts, yes. As I said before, child. I can't help it, when you're right beside me, practically yelling in my ear. But you may give the fish as a little present to your sister. I imagine your father can make her a bowl to keep him in, something more interesting than a plain old jar.'

'I'm sorry…' Mariana whispered. 'I didn't mean to be rude.'

'Nor did I.' He smiled at her as he dipped his gnarled fingers into the bowl, and stirred. 'As you suspected, I don't have many people to talk to. Most of the city hurries past my door as fast as they can.'

'Even the children?' Mariana frowned. 'Even when you make such beautiful things, like this fish, and the birds I saw fly out from under the arches before?'

'They lurk around the portico, and peer inside. Dare each other to run and stick a toe over the threshold. But very few ever come right in.'

'I would.' Mariana sighed. 'There aren't any shops like this on the island. I've never seen anyone do this sort of magic. Why are you mixing it with your hands like that?'

'Your father breathes magic into his creations, I have to touch.' He lifted his fingers out, stained purplish with the mixture. 'Pass me that little green glass bottle there.'

Mariana handed it to him, and the old man cupped his hands, whispering. Then he poured a fragrant violet liquid out from between his fingers into the bottle, stoppered it swiftly, and handed it back to Mariana.

'It smells of berries!' She stared at his hands, and then at the bowl, all perfectly clean.

'You said she wanted it to taste nice.'

'What will it do?' Mariana asked, cradling the tiny bottle between her palms.

The magician closed his hand over hers, and sighed. 'Not enough. I wish I could do more, but it will help. A little more life inside her. Less pain. Quieter sleep.'

'That's more than I hoped for,' Mariana murmured, but she could feel her eyes filling with tears. This was magic she believed in. If Signor Nesso had told her Eliza would recover, she would have trusted him – far more than any of the other travelling mages, with their outlandish claims. She trusted him now, when he said that he couldn't mend her sister. That no one could. It felt like the beginning of goodbye.